A Legend of WOLF SONG

A Legend of WOLF SONG

As told by
GEORGE STONE

Illustrated by Dick Kramer

Publishers Grosset & Dunlap New York

Published simultaneously in Canada
Library of Congress catalog card number: 74-24673
ISBN 0-448-11879-3
First printing
Printed in the United States of America

For the wolf and his natural world.
Free, true, and altogether good.

For Igor and Lācis.

And because of Friday.

Prologue

The ageless sky was waiting above crisp, snow-dusted landscape. Waiting in silence. Breathless. Then it came, imperceptibly—with no precise beginning. Eerie fluting music. Strange siren sounds rising briefly, then trailing in long, tonal streams weaving into the night. Now a mingling of throaty, fluid refrains pulsing in mysterious chorale. Echoing from indefinable distance and direction. As the voices of time itself. The wolves were singing.

To hear the song of the wolf is to experience a singularly moving sensual expression of wilderness. Sound of unreachable quality, seeming weird and inhuman. But not unearthly. For it is of the essence of the creature wolf: of his spirit, his being, his truth. A transcendental song that took form uncounted millennia before time was defined. Something elemental. A living call from the past. A revelation of the very Universe.

And yet it is legend that for part of their history, wolves did not sing. This is a story of how the wolf lost and then regained the freedom of his soul.

The Wolf sang for the Mountain, who was proud.
The Wolf sang for All.

His Song was of Love.
For Earth. For Life.
The Truth of his Soul. An endless stream.
Ancient even before the Ice came.
In the time of Dirus, the Great Dire Wolf.

He who has not such Love cannot sing.
And will call Song evil. Unwolfly.
Thus was Rufus. Rufus, the tyrant wolf. The destroyer.
He and his believers took Song away.
And for eons the Sky was empty.

But the stream flowed on. Joining Past and Future.
Dirus returned.
His search was long. But sure.
For the Spirit lived, waiting.
Released, its Power surged.
Again the Wolf was free. The Earth whole.

The Wolf sings for the Mountain, who is proud.
The Wolf sings for All.

—A Legend

ONE

Wolf trotted confidently along just below the ridge-crest. His muzzle was low, inhaling stories of the earth, while his eyes casually searched ahead as dogs' eyes will, peering from side to side over the frames of invisible glasses. Soon he paused and raised his nose to sample the breeze curling over the hill. The smells of other wolves were heady. Waves of excitement played through his taut body, hair bristling on his shoulders, along his spine.

He resumed his weaving course through the sagebrush and angled up toward a rocky knoll atop the ridge. He stopped abruptly at the scent of a bobcat. It was old. The rubble of rocks was dark and shadowy in starlight. With an effortless bound of ten feet, he stood on a flat boulder at the high point. Ears erect, tail down, he surveyed the slopes below. Wolf knew this country well; he had been whelped in a den less than a mile away. His long, stilt-like legs were trembling. He momentarily glanced over his shoulder at the crescent moon. Then he sat. For a long time he breathed deeply, eyes half-closed. But he could not relax. His muscles tensed and quivered.

Slowly his head arced upward, ears back. His jaws parted slightly as his lips cupped forward. And for the very first time, he began to sing. Lowly and nervously. The air seemed to still as his voice rose, and his entire consciousness poured into his song. It stirred his spirit as nothing ever had. He was at once eager and afraid, ecstatic and melancholy. But the compulsion that drove him was absolute. And he gave himself to the night.

Down ridges and gullies onto the plains, over foothills into mountain valleys, his long notes rose and fell. They gave a new sensation to the living earth—powerful, sensuous, timeless. A vole scurrying through grass in the ravine below jerked to a halt and stood on its tiny hind feet, whiskers twitching.

Three young coyotes in wide rank ranged upwind across the sage flats, hoping to jump a jackrabbit. As the night breeze lulled, Wolf's far-off song came to them. Although barely audible and mellowed by distance, it had the effect of a lightning bolt. In unison they froze with cocked head and raised forepaw. No brother's call that! They shuddered in fear of the unknown.

A bull elk grazing three miles distant swept his huge head upward. Motionless, he listened. His lungs inflated reflexively in preparation for reply. But this was not the voice of his kind—nor of any other he knew. Strange, yet—somehow familiar. Certainly not the yapping wail of a coyote, nor the scream of a cougar. This was the profound expression of a very different soul, a very ancient soul. He turned slowly and trotted toward a nearby herd. He did not know quite why.

Wolf's confidence grew steadily. Each phrase he sustained longer, achieving greater volume and wider range. He was surprised by his talent and its natural facility. He seemed to learn instinctively from each new effort—as though virtuosity had been his before, dormant but not forgotten. And yet he had never heard a wolf sing! In fact, he had learned early the universal contempt of his kind for such unintelligent expression, such undignified exhibitionism. Especially for the bellicose shoutings and raucous screechings of that most vulgar of races, the coyotes.

His full voice pealed across the prairie—rich and

free. Shivers scintillated through his body producing tremolo. An ethereal siren. Repressed guilt and revulsion departed his being, for he felt the harmony of his music with the night. He became intoxicated, inspired. He knew that it was right, his right, his fulfillment. He knew it. He felt it in his soul. So he sang and sang.

Fresh scents in the air failed to penetrate his concentration. Eyelids still tightly closed, he recalled his visions of Dirus, the Great Dire Wolf. The gray giant whose aloof majesty compels respect and faith. Whose shocking and incredible revelations could only be accepted and believed. Wolf had been awed by this exotic, distant creature since their first meeting. He knew a spiritual bond with him. Now he sensed physical kinship and strained to summon him. He craved approval. His effort was so desperate that he lost equilibrium, nearly toppling from his rock. Eyes again open, ears erect, he was instantly aware that he was surrounded by wolves.

As he breathed in and met the eyes of a young dog below him, several others bared their teeth and growled threateningly. Wolf rose to all fours, hackles up. He was humping his back in a slow stretch when an old bitch hit him from behind, tearing fur and flesh from his haunch. He fell sprawling among the rocks. Wolf was a large dog entering his prime, more than equal to physical challenge by most of his peers. He regained his feet just as four wolves closed on him.

Wheeling to his rear, he caught a forepaw of the bitch and flipped her to her back. He lunged for her throat, and she folded her legs in submission. Another bitch and two dogs moved in. Wolf sprang to a commanding boulder and glared down at them, amber eyes burning. They held.

He had expected hostility, but knowing made it no easier for him to have to defend himself against his own kind for the first time in his life. It ran counter to his very nature and grieved him deeply. Wolf loved his own. He struck his most impressive, full-chested pose and voiced a final plaintive call. It seemed sadder and more personal than before. For a brief time, his attackers hesitated, listening. The young dog even lay down and placed his head between forepaws. But the trance was broken by a low growl from the old bitch, and they circled to Wolf's rear. Eleven other wolves were there now. They would force him to run.

Wolf could not survive a fight with so many. He did not want to fight. He had only wanted them to listen. He knew that his adversaries would delay their attack until he ended his song and noticed them. So he broke his pattern, cutting off abruptly, and leapt fifteen feet to the base of the rocks. He was running flat out as soon as he landed. The split second gained by surprise plus his unusual speed and stamina would see him safely away. He sped up the ridgecrest toward the foothills, hurdling rocks with the grace of a deer. His heavy gray and cream coat rippled in the faint light and flowed back and forth over his sinewy frame. The others were strung out behind, the closest some twenty yards back and losing ground.

Two wolves suddenly appeared ahead and began accelerating on both sides of him. Wolf put on an extra burst of speed as if intending to run by them. Then, without breaking stride, he lowered his head and rammed the wolf on the right full in the ribs with the momentum of 120 pounds behind his shoulders. The mature bitch was knocked flat and struggled to regain her breath. Wolf spun 180 degrees in mid-air and vaulted toward the second wolf, feinting a frontal charge. As the other backed and maneuvered for defense, Wolf turned sharply aside and raced on up the ridge, now only five yards ahead of his leading pursuer. He was tiring but still had much in reserve. He pushed himself, exulting in his speed and strength. His legs stretched horizontally as he flew over the sage and pulled away. By the time he reached the head of the ridge and swept onto a broad flat at the base of the foothills, he knew that he was no longer being followed.

Slowing to a lope, Wolf scented a group of pronghorns. He veered into the wind directly toward them, again pressing to top speed. It was one of those rare, lucky accidents. His approach had been so sudden that he was actually passing the startled sentry when it issued its first snort of alarm and bolted. The rest of the herd was barely on its feet when Wolf burst upon them. The frightened antelope, white rumps flaring, milled in confusion before streaking off to his left. He could easily have bowled over any one of at least three does, but his mind was not on a kill.

He swung alongside the trailing buck and nipped his flank just for effect. The terrified pronghorns soon reached 45 miles per hour, leaving Wolf far behind. But still he ran, testing his endurance. His spirit soared. He had never felt so exhilarated, liberated. Reborn. Finally nearing exhaustion, he stopped and stood panting heavily a long while. He gazed at the mountains. He would go to them and send his voice echoing down their valleys. Other wolves must know the joy of song: their heritage, the essence of their identity. He looked toward the site of his struggle five miles back. He was restless with purpose and resolve. He raised his head to the stars and sang with unimaginable feeling. This, he realized, was the beginning of his real life.

TWO

It was an exceptionally crisp dawn for early fall. Stars were awash in the pale gray of first light on the eastern horizon. Wolf was lying tightly curled, his bushy tail protecting his nose. Fog from his breath drifted slowly over his shoulders and up the gully. Although his eyes were closed, he was not asleep. He was beginning to feel thirst and hunger, and he remembered the pronghorns which he had so casually bypassed in his excitement a few hours before. He would visit a stream in the mouth of a nearby canyon and then try his luck

at an early-morning hunt. He hoped that he would be able to rest much of the day. He tried to suppress gnawing disappointment at the results of his first efforts and think instead of the future. Surely the power of his song would reach other wolves. Perhaps the young dog who lay down and listened would break away and join him—and learn. But Wolf was not without doubts. He wondered if others knew, if others had tried. Was he the first to hold communion with the past, or was he just one of many destined to be frustrated by the impossible—an inspired but naive dreamer?

The wound in his right thigh was throbbing when the pungent smell of a Plains grizzly welled over him. Wolf leapt to his feet, senses straining. Where is it? Where is it moving? He trotted rigidly up to a better vantage point. The scent came around the hill in front of him—the bear had crossed below. Wolf scanned all within his view but detected no movement. His heart pounded; stiffness ebbed from his limbs. He was startled but not afraid. The great beast was a threat only in surprise at close quarters.

Wolf walked cautiously back downslope toward the mouth of the gully. Near the base he intersected the bear's trail. It was very fresh. The stench was oppressive to his sensitive nose. To improve the situation, he delicately lifted his leg and urinated on a clump of particularly offensive rabbit brush. That seemed to ease the ache in his haunch. He was grateful for not having to bear such repugnant body odor himself even to gain such immense strength. Another scent, almost masked, was there too. Had the bear been trailing bison? No! Wolf's stomach contracted and gurgled as he recognized the visceral smell of a recently killed cow buffalo. The grizzly had just been feeding! Wolf scampered across the arroyo and galloped eagerly along the backtrail, his tongue lolling in anticipation.

The dead bison was at the edge of a bluff three miles up the valley. She lay on her back with her head twisted around, staring forward. Her skull had been crushed by a tremendous drive. The back legs dangled to each side from a broken pelvis. The bear had emptied her body cavity and also eaten much from one hindquarter. Wolf gorged himself on warm meat and blood, trying to ignore the strong grizzly smell. Now he would not have to concern himself with hunting for the better part of a week.

The sun was rising. A breeze flowed freshly in Wolf's face as he paused, feeling full and sluggish. His right ear rotated backward. Had that been the rattle of gravel? His pads felt the earth shaking. As he turned his head, his eye flashed the image of a hulking shadow bearing down on him, and his nose cringed in a cloud of fetid ursine breath. In desperation, Wolf flung himself across the bison carcass, almost avoiding the sweep of a gigantic paw tipped with claws five inches long.

The blow grazed Wolf's shoulder, spinning him ten feet into the air—and over the bluff. He cascaded out of control down the shale scree onto a grassy flat below. The irate grizzly, not well designed for a downhill charge, lumbered after him, bellowing loudly. Wolf scrambled to his feet, slightly stunned, and limped as quickly as he could up the valley. The bear had no reason to follow.

Notwithstanding his debt to the bear for a free meal, this was not the way Wolf had hoped to start the day. With two sore legs, he would not be able to rely on speed for protection. He must be careful and use his head. He promised himself never again to stand facing the wind, unguarded and ill-alert. He skirted a clump of willows and followed a game path diagonally to the crest of a low divide. He could already smell water on the far side. In a moment he stood on the creek bank. As was his habit, he sprang to a midstream bar, but his bruised foreleg crumpled, somersaulting him painfully onto his back. A spasm of dizziness and nausea engulfed him, but it passed. He rolled over to his side and lay there panting, stretched out on the sand. He was beginning to wonder if fate had now turned against him. Was the mission he felt so strongly only foolish fancy, in violation of the natural order of things?

Wolf pulled himself up, moved to the water's edge, and drank long and deliberately. He then tiptoed distastefully across a riffle and ambled upstream along

the bank. A Steller's jay shrieked its warning from a nearby cottonwood. Wolf stopped to watch some cutthroat trout lying near the bottom of a still pool. A delicacy he had tasted once as a puppy. He wished that somehow he could share their love of swimming. Movement on the water drew his attention—his own reflection. Piercing almond eyes; quasi-hypnotic. His body relaxed as he stared at the image. A puff of wind stirred cottonwood leaves and blurred the water. Wolf's head and shoulders seemed to grow larger, more massive, darker. As the ripples subsided, the metamorphosed visage remained. His heart boomed—he was looking into the eyes of the Great Dire Wolf!

Wolf trembled but could not move—paralyzed as upon waking from a terrifying dream. His fear was not of physical danger but of the mysterious—a spiritual breach of time beyond his comprehension—and of the profound importance and uncertainty of his future. He felt utterly inadequate. Dirus wanted to know if Wolf had sung. Yes. Had he learned that song was the purest expression of his soul, his life? Yes, but . . . but others had not. Wolf questioned whether they could, their animosity had been so immediate and extreme. He thought that he had performed well, but he had failed in his first attempt. Perhaps his ability was inadequate.

Dirus was displeased. Had he not forewarned Wolf that he must be prepared for endless frustration, that his resolve must be unshakable? Did Wolf not realize that even one success would be the greatest achievement for wolves in uncounted millennia? Did he not understand that once the spirit of free expression was again released, it would never lie dormant? That it would rejuvenate the primal instincts of his kind, rekindle wolves' racial pride, reestablish their dignity and nobility?

Wolf had thought that he understood. He longed to believe. But his luck suddenly seemed to have turned bad—and there were so many unanswered questions. If only he could know more, he was sure that his faith would be stronger. Dirus was obviously impatient. The surface of the pool shimmered, diffusing his bold countenance. No, wait! I want to understand, to know. The water stilled, and Dirus' great eyes emitted new power, penetrating Wolf's mind to the core of his soul. You can only understand and know when your faith becomes infinite, invincible. That is within you. I cannot give it to you. If you commit yourself totally, you shall find it. Let no bite of a bitch nor bruise from a bear discourage you. Such trivial events are of no importance! Clearly the Great Dire Wolf knew all that had happened.

Wolf was under the other's control: he knew that Dirus was right—and would always prevail. He trusted him, but there was much that he did not comprehend. If song had been a natural and universal creation of his kind, then how could it ever have been taken away, lost? How could any wolf have imposed his will on the future, sterilizing the spirit of his own? Why and how did Rufus do this?

Wolf felt that he should close his eyes, clear his mind. He sighed and waited, losing consciousness of all that his senses constantly told him. Sunlight through his eyelids produced a reddish brown background. It became mottled, and color concentrated around many centers. One spot near the middle grew as the others darkened. In kaleidoscopic animation, the form of an animal gradually took shape. A rust-colored wolf pup, a young dog. Other puppies and adults were scattered about the scene, some sitting, some standing. The reddish one appeared to be much larger and more powerfully built than his littermates. Wolf knew that this was Rufus.

To Wolf's astonishment, a mature dog on the left raised his muzzle skyward and sang—beautifully. With more control than he himself had yet developed. He pressed his eyelids more tightly shut and watched intently. Several other wolves sang in turn. Then one, two—all of the puppies joined in a yapping, yodeling chorus, attempting to emulate their elders. All save one, that is. Rufus barked and growled but did not sing. Soon, the red-brown pup lowered its head and, ears back, skulked out of view. Rufus could not sing!

It took a few seconds for Wolf's eyes to refocus. Dirus was still with him. Wolf did not know quite how to interpret what he had seen. If Rufus had been unable to sing, and singing had been enjoyed so much by other wolves, then how could Rufus possibly have changed them? By force! Violence! Dirus was suddenly angry, his broad head shaking with harnessed rage. Wolf became more apprehensive. He hesitated before inquiring further. He still could not imagine how such freedom and joy could be muted. And if that had occurred, then how could he, Wolf, regenerate the past merely by persuasion and example? Because it lives within you! In the souls of all wolves. It cannot be destroyed. You must draw it out, once again to excite and enrich the night and the day, the sky and the earth!

Wolf was panting. He could see his own tongue on the water. Dirus was gone. After each meeting Wolf felt more inspired and comprehended more. But just as his determination was steeled, so his curiosity was heightened. More and more unanswered questions. Exactly how had Rufus been able to deprive wolves of their natural expression and fulfillment by force? Had his influence truly been universal? Why? And how could it have lasted so long? How had Dirus come from the distant past? Was Wolf the first and only instrument of his crusade? And why he? Most challenging and disturbing of all, could he possibly accomplish the enormous task that Dirus expected? But in spite of his ignorance and transitory doubts,

Wolf was ever more certain of the meaning of his existence.

His brain was buzzing. His injuries ached. On a whim, he jumped headlong into the deep pool and dove until he felt his forepaws plunge into muddy ooze on the bottom. He kept himself submerged, opening his eyes in the cool water. It was turbid with swirling mud and moss. The trout had departed. Somewhat refreshed, he climbed onto the opposite bank and shook his body vigorously from head to tail, showering the surroundings with spray and ending with a stylish posterior flourish. Wolf looked up at the graying sky. Two mergansers were strenuously winging their way toward the mountains.

Rustle, rustle, plop! In the grass. He pinned the frog with a deft thrust of his right forepaw and gulped down an unexpected dessert. He was still full—and tired, mentally and physically. He noticed a ledge in the valley wall ahead and trotted toward it, unconsciously sniffing the ground. As he curled up at the base of the rocks, Wolf thought of the coming night. He must test his home pack again. From over the hill at his back, the wind brought scents and sounds to his ever-active nose and ears. He slept.

THREE

The night was dark under low clouds. Big feathery snowflakes rode the upslope wind. Wolf was sleeping fitfully, his lips and eyes twitching, his legs jerking in subconscious chase. On strong silent wings, a great horned owl glided by within three feet of him. He sensed the bird's presence and awakened, following it with his ears. Rising stiffly, he shook an inch of snow from his fur and luxuriated in a series of long, slow stretches. After a few sniffs and quick glances into the gloom, Wolf trotted back across the valley, diagonally into the wind. He favored his right foreleg; the shoulder was swollen and sore. But he felt good, well fed and well rested. And he loved the snow. He had as long as he could remember—much to the consternation of some of the older wolves. He let the soft flakes fly into his open mouth, occasionally snapping at them in playful delight.

Nearly an hour later Wolf stood below the foothills where he had stampeded the pronghorns. He nuzzled and pawed the fluffy white blanket, hoping to uncover the history of his antelope adventure. After considerable circling and crisscrossing, he found the place and immediately rolled onto his back, wriggling and kicking in the upside-down canine dance. He stopped and looked around mischievously. A large snowflake hit him in the eye. That triggered more inverted gyrations—great fun. But he knew that he was stalling. He would reverse his course of the previous night, approaching the wolf ridge upwind. Finally he righted himself, shook, and started off.

Above all, Wolf had to keep a protective distance. He was nervous and couldn't quite decide on an appropriate spot. The rim of a shallow amphitheatre at the head of a gully—an easy escape route. He squinted into the blowing snow. It seemed to be letting up. He seated himself, carefully adjusting his position, and closed his eyes. Concentrate. He felt an urge growing within him, excitement building, pounding. And for the second night, the earth heard his voice.

This time he needed to warm up, practice, reassure himself. His first attempts were rather meek and private. But confidence rushed back. Inhaling deeply, he reached for a bold crescendo of volume and feeling. His song flowed over the hills, subduing the swirling snow. Again and again he explored the limits of his magnificent gift. Ten thousand creatures of the prairie listened in wonder. It was frightening—but not dreadful; without reason, it seemed fitting and good. Thrilling.

Wolf held his breath to hear the last notes return and fade. His moist black nose scrutinized the air currents. A musky badger—somewhere near. Wolves' smells were there, but the animals were not moving. Would they simply ignore his call? He doubted that. Not after their earlier reaction. Perhaps he should move, keep his whereabouts uncertain. No, he had time enough for that. And the storm was subsiding. Once more his voice pierced the night. An impassioned plea—over and over. He strained and squeezed all that he could give. As his eyelids parted, he saw stars through breaking clouds. Wolves were coming. Now he must move.

The old bitch was furious as she led seven wolves up the ridge. (Others were away hunting, taking advantage of the silencing snow, playing the wind.) Such degrading violation of nature must be suppressed. Most aberrant behavior was merely destructive of respect and rank, but this was fundamentally immoral. Not healthy independence and rebellion, but overt, flaunted blasphemy—depravity. The willful act of a corrupted, criminal wolf. A dog in her troop paused to mark a boulder. She turned. One look told him that feeding scent to the wind was stupid. They all waited, listening. Her plan was to circle beyond the hated one, to put him upwind.

A mile to the north, Wolf sang again. Once. Twice. Enough. He was standing, ready to run. He shifted his weight and peered thoughtfully into the darkness. Why this emptiness, this hollow loneliness? Why had he to fear his brethren for whose love and companionship he longed? Despite his commitment, in his heart he knew that he was no loner. He didn't want to be. Why are they blind to the beauty of life? If only one could see. One kindred spirit. One other voice. In the reality of mortal danger, Dirus seemed so very far away—so hopelessly remote and inaccessible. Unreal. The odor of canine urine drifted to him. They're close. Wolf could not let them outflank him downwind.

The young wolf trailed the pack. He was not at all enthusiastic. He had wanted to go hunting, to have a chance to prove himself. This excursion seemed silly and unnecessary. Stalking another wolf! He would have looked for elk, tested a herd. There, a straying, sickly calf. Charge! His gangling dark-gray body sprang into action. He closed rapidly and prepared to leap for the quarry's rump. But his imagined triumph was shattered by a sound. The voice of that wolf! The others veered to the right and broke into a gallop. The young dog stopped to listen. A second call came. He had been taught that it was evil, and yet—it appealed to him. He liked it. He felt that it was directed to him. Incomprehensibly, a personal message. An important message.

Wolf was limping up a spur toward the foothills when he heard the young dog bark. The breeze brought it clearly. At first he thought it was a coyote. But his nose rejected that. Several yips and yaps, then an oscillating, quavering sort of moan. Wolf trembled with excitement. Staring at infinity, he turned his ears to the best angle. Another series of barks and a sincere if inadequate wail. The young dog knows! It is within him! Wolf must wait, forget his own safety. All at once he was warm and happy, elated, consumed by optimism and faith. He cried out encouragement. The young dog would come. He had to. Wolf waited and hoped.

The reply was peculiar. Erratic, high-pitched, almost—desperate. A strange imitation of song. For a time Wolf refused to recognize what his ears registered. Not yelps of pain and terror. Not a puppy's protestations to harsh discipline. The scent of fear came . . . and Wolf knew the bitter disappointment of success briefly tasted, then lost. Rufus was at work, destroying a free spirit. Wolf agonized in the knowledge that another—and his first potential ally—was paying a price for his deeds. If only he could have helped. Yet he realized that the young dog's sacrifice had given him time to escape. He moved on—unconsciously, dejectedly. As though having awakened uncertainly after an ill-remembered bad experience, he had a terribly depressing feeling that something awful had happened.

Without design, he walked to the mountains. They stood massive and white against the night sky.

FOUR

Clouds of mist were rising from beaver ponds toward the pale blue sky. A belted kingfisher chittered its way upstream. It was a brilliant, clean morning. Beyond the water, wapiti were scattered across a great meadow of white and gold. To the west, snowcapped monoliths rose salmon orange in the early sun. Presently a mild chinook wind hushed down the broad valley, streaming fresh snow from the tops of towering pines.

Wolf viewed this scene from the edge of an aspen cluster at the base of the valley wall. A beautiful, sensuous adagio. Its calm splendor soothed him. Quaking and rustling in the breeze, round leaves above his head shook off their crystal coats, dusting the tips of his fur with snow. The aspen were beginning to turn: clumps of pastel greens and golden yellows. Wolf's appreciation of his world was singular, a powerful, pervasive force in his makeup. He drew strength and purpose from it. His feelings were innocent and honest, simple but profound. They coursed through him in a vitalizing wave. Erect and solid, he held his head high, muzzle slightly upward. Sighing deeply, he watched the cloud of fog that flowed from his nostrils.

From the corner of his eye, Wolf saw motion. Aspen branches shaking and swaying. Then a cracking, and they disappeared. The beaver had not detected him and was indiscreetly far from the safety of his pond. Without a thought, Wolf began his stalk. The chunky rodent was attentively snipping branches from the new-fallen tree. But soft snow failed to silence the dead leaves as Wolf padded forward, and the beaver was warned. He humped toward an arm of the nearest pond as quickly as his webbed feet could carry him.

Wolf leapt into full gallop, obliquely intersecting and blocking his quarry's path ten feet from the water. The beaver was so intent upon reaching the pond that he nearly collided with Wolf, who slumped down on forepaws in a sort of playful bow and snapped at the beaver's legs. But the other was defending his life, not of a mind to play. From a crouch, he lunged at Wolf's throat with his huge tree-gouging incisors. Wolf was taken aback, almost insulted by this potentially lethal rebuke. Cautiously, he circled the beaver who, propped upright by his paddle tail, rotated slowly to face the danger. As Wolf crossed the other's backtrail, the beaver lurched toward his pond. And Wolf let him go, merely trotting behind and sniffing.

The beaver plunged into the ice-fringed water with a prodigious splash, and Wolf watched him disappear before a wake of bubbles. He surfaced near the middle of the pond and, rolling like a furry porpoise, smacked the water loudly with his tail. This action he dutifully repeated at regular intervals. Soon Wolf heard other splashes around the far side of the pond. The entire colony had been alerted to his presence.

He turned to his left and ducked into a tunnel-like passage through some willows, emerging at the end of the beaver dam. He could have proceeded straight to his destination but instead strode out across the dam itself. The pond was not high; most of the outflow was leaking through the dam below. Wolf ambled along nonchalantly, enjoying the crossing like a child conquering a wall. He glanced over at the beaver house with an obvious air of superiority. But near the far end he lost his footing on the slippery sticks and, to his embarrassment, found his hindquarters draped in a most undignified fashion down the front of the dam. He scrambled back up, jumped the final twelve feet to the bank and, without looking back, galloped off into the trees.

As Wolf approached the edge of the stream to drink, his nose registered wolf scent. The trail of a single wolf crossed the fresh snow on a mudbank in front of him. He raced back and forth, sniffing the tracks excitedly. Made by an old dog. Forgetting his mild thirst, he abruptly darted back into the trees. The trail led through a scattered stand of mature lodgepole pines and up to the top of a moraine ridge. Wolf loped along the ridgecrest, eager to meet his fellow. He could not have passed more than a few hours earlier.

After a mile of winding through boulder-strewn timber, Wolf burst into an open park. Thump! Thump! Thump! Two young mule deer bucks bounded up the brushy slopes above. Wolf knew they were there without looking. But he ignored them—he had lost the old wolf's trail.

Circling frantically, he soon picked it up again—veering off to the right and downslope. Now in a denser forest, he had to thread his way carefully through the tangle of deadfall. Before long he caught flashing glimpses of the valley floor between the thinning pines. Upon reaching the edge of the trees, he paused. Far below, the old wolf was hurrying awkwardly across a grassy meadow toward the stream. He was fleeing Wolf.

Wolf studied the terrain, planning his pursuit. He watched the old one until he was lost to view among willows along the creek. Then, in apparent disinterest, he sat and scratched his neck and shoulder vigorously. It felt good. A second time. He knew that he could overtake the other wolf at will. A Fremont squirrel announced its presence from a nearby Douglas fir. Wolf turned his head in acknowledgment. Then he sprang downhill.

Once across the talus, he bounced to the bottom and ran upvalley half a mile. As in response to a signal, he swerved to the right and streaked toward a beaver dam. Crossing this one in seconds, he doubled back downstream and lay flat in the grass.

The old wolf limped up the bank and trotted across a terrace, ears to the rear, nose up. Although in a hurry, he stopped short, unable to move. He sensed danger and was helpless. Wolf finally rose to confront him. But not in challenge. He did not try to stare the older one down, which would have been easy, but instead turned his head aside in a gesture of submission. The elder trembled. He did not understand this abnormal reaction.

In a moment Wolf met his eyes again, advanced a few steps, then lowered his head. He wanted desperately to gain the other's confidence. The old wolf stopped shaking and circled slowly to the right. He looked straight ahead, eschewing direct visual contact, acting out the transparent ritual of disdain and unconcern. Wolf rolled onto his back and thrashed the air jerkily with his paws, as though playing by the family den. The old one was nonplussed. This approach was beyond his experience, which was considerable. Wolf was a strong, large dog who could have forced complete submission immediately. What could he possibly want? He must have some peculiar purpose. Or be deranged. Yet, there was no sign of the madness.

Retreating could only prolong the ordeal. Hackles raised, the old dog sprang to catch his pursuer off guard. Wolf easily rolled out of reach and flipped himself upright, ready to repel the attack. But the elder just stood there: panting, staring uncertainly. Wolf returned his gaze, sat, and gently batted at him with a forepaw. After a moment, the old one glanced about at the snow-covered ground and also sat down. Then he looked again into those penetrating, urgent eyes. What do you want?

A companion. An ally! The old wolf was no less puzzled. Why? At your age, in your condition, why aren't you an accepted member of a group—even a leader? Why join me, a weak old outcast who won't see another warm season?

The whistling scream of a red-tailed hawk punctuated the question. Wolf looked skyward as the bird's shadow swept by. Without hesitation he answered in full voice. It was by far the best he had ever achieved with no warmup. A sustained, then trailing chorus that crossed and recrossed the valley, at once an assertion of determination and a primal appeal. The tingling that spread from his spine was by now familiar but still thrilling—and surprising. He did not hurry his song but let it fade naturally. When he looked down and refocused, the old wolf was sitting like a bewildered puppy: ears erect, head cocked to one side. He conveyed only blank amazement. The hawk was flying and almost out of sight.

Wolf raised his muzzle slightly, holding the other's gaze, and sang again—lowly. With exquisite control. Although relieved that the old one had not manifested hostility or fright, he was asking for some reaction. Elder, have you ever heard a wolf sing? A pause.

Only puppies, but I didn't consider it singing—whatever you mean by that. More like squealing. And then it was done innocently, probably in imitation of coyotes. Never intentionally, and never more than once or twice. They were silenced immediately. I myself helped to educate one such pup to the ways of wolves. But you, you disgrace your kind on purpose!

Why do you think of song as disgrace?

Because it is unnatural for wolves. It is an alien practice: ignoble and demeaning.

These thoughts once again upset Wolf. I do not

find it unnatural. It is honest, beautiful expression. I am able to do it; I want to do it. Therefore, it must be natural.

No! It is *un*natural, perverted, and immoral. A debasing act of lower creatures, coyotes.

Wolf had been aware of these beliefs as long as he could remember. Always expressed in the same tiresome way. Part of the wolf's creed. But he now knew them to be mindless notions: contrary to his own experience, belied by his knowledge of the past.

His eyes blazed with conviction. Elder, what you believe is untrue. Song is not immoral for it is harmless. More than that, it is uplifting, self-releasing—pure pleasure. Can you not feel how good it is for me? And I am certain that it can be a very effective and satisfying way for wolves to communicate.

The old wolf was revolted. He had never been exposed to such undisguised heresy. He considered ignoring Wolf and simply walking away. But the power of the other's presence prevailed; Wolf's eyes fixed him. And Wolf rose to the occasion—his first chance to express his beliefs to another living wolf. He was highly stimulated. Ideas which he had never organized streamed forth.

It is not unnatural for me. You heard. Apparently it is not unnatural for puppies. Those you heard trying to sing must have done so naturally. Do they imitate the bull elk or the golden eagle? No! Neither do they imitate the coyote. They vent what is born in them—and has been from time immemorial. Have you never questioned your beliefs? Are they innate, or were they taught you? Singing is no more unnatural for wolves now than it was for our ancient ancestors at a time when all wolves sang freely and happily—and led fuller lives. What *is* unnatural, what *is* immoral is the suppression and destruction of a beautiful part of wolves' experience!

Wolf was aroused. (And he knew that Dirus was proud of him.) Elder was stunned. He had not thought about other than his daily needs for so long that he could barely cope with the flood of thoughts flashing through his mind. Still staring into the dominating eyes of his companion, he finally regathered his wits. Wolf was either insane indeed, or somehow enlightened and inspired. How can you possibly know what—what happened in the past?

Wolf hesitated. He wanted Elder to understand, but he feared rejection. The sun was quite high; a few cottony clouds were puffing up over the peaks. Melting snow fed trickles of water that cascaded musically down to the stream. It has come to my mind. I have seen and heard it. Dirus has shown me how it was, how it changed, how it should be again.

Who is Dirus?

Dirus—the Great Dire Wolf. A huge, wise wolf

from the very distant past. He seems to know everything that has ever happened.

A delta-shaped fly lit on Elder's gray-black nose. In his clumsy haste to brush it off, he tumbled over in the slushy snow—and ate a few mouthfuls. He was suddenly at ease. Wolf remained intensely serious. Dirus from the distant past, eh? You're sure he wasn't a product of too many fermented berries?

Wolf was annoyed at first. Now I suppose you accuse me of mimicking a mountain grizzly! But then he relaxed. He realized that he had won a friend, if a somewhat skeptical one. He felt like singing. So he did.

FIVE

Wolf liked mouthfuls of fresh snow. Its light coolness felt good on his tongue. But he much preferred cold stream water to slake his thirst. Elder sat on the bluff as Wolf went down to drink. He drank more than he really needed, all the while peering up at his new-found companion. The old wolf was in poor condition: thin and weak. He must be very hungry.

Wolf rejoined him. Let's look over that herd of elk farther down the valley. Elder needed no time to consider this proposition and immediately fell into line behind Wolf as he trotted toward the trees. Beyond a low ridge, they descended a ravine and followed a small tributary around to its confluence with the main stream. This maneuver put them below the elk meadow, downwind and undetected.

White water was exploding over boulder-studded rapids. Spray shimmered with rainbow colors in shafts of sunlight that penetrated overhanging boughs of blue spruce. Wolf and Elder filed through cool, green shadows and bridged the thundering torrent on an immense dead trunk. Water droplets tickled their noses. Brushing lush wet foliage, they clambered upslope to a knoll from which they could reconnoiter the meadow. Most of the elk were on the far side in and near the trees. Many had bedded down. The two wolves watched for a few moments, then trotted off to the left, circling the open grassland out of sight in the forest.

About two hundred yards from the nearest elk, they stopped for a tactical conference. Wolf would enter the field openly, traversing it between the elk in the trees and some others scattered farther out to the right. Elder would wait. Tails wagging, they touched noses in a toast to good fortune.

Wolf was a consummate actor. He strolled through the shoulder-high grass totally oblivious to his immediate surroundings. Dreaming of some far-off destination, his journey was guided solely by basic geometry—the shortest distance being a straight line.

His course kept him about fifty yards from elk, roughly equidistant on both sides. Most of the big deer were aware of him, but few took alarm. Some moved slowly away. Several calves ran to their mothers. But Wolf completely ignored these movements. Studied disinterest. The Great Divide beckoned him onward.

His nose soon confirmed what furtive glances had suggested. A foolish bullcalf on the right was separated from its mother. It was ready to risk a dash to the trees. Wolf was ready too.

The anxious cow, however, was not taken in by Wolf's thespian talents. Without ceremony, she charged. Having little time to spare, Wolf swerved aside and reversed his course, tail comfortably tucked between his hind legs. The play had ended. Sharply pointed hooves driven by six hundred pounds of instinctive maternal fury seemed more compelling than the relief of Elder's hunger. He raced directly away from the endangered calf, knowing that the cow would quickly return to it.

This gave Elder a rare opportunity to be smug and critical. But he was not. Wolf had made a good try—and for him. Besides, he had news. An enfeebled old cow is lying up just a hundred yards to the left. Elder's plan would afford him the satisfaction of helping to secure his own food.

Wolf moved with utmost stealth, placing himself at the edge of a clearing not far behind the old cow—

and downwind. Elder, feeling the pride of a thousand hunts, limped exaggeratedly into the meadow. When directly opposite his prey, the wily old predator began sniffing the ground excitedly, zigzagging back and forth parallel to the forest fringe. Continuing this performance, he advanced closer and closer to the increasingly nervous cow.

At last she rose and galloped away in panic. Wolf's timing was good, but his enthusiasm somewhat excessive. He nearly jumped right over her, landing full in the saddle of her back. She crumpled under the impact. All knew that it was the natural end of her life. She would be spared endless months of parasitic deterioration and starvation.

Elder had not fed so well in two years. Wolf let him finish his feast before he himself partook. The two drank long from the stream. They returned to the elk carcass for a perfunctory sniffing and then walked uphill to rest in the shade of a bushy limber pine. Elder slept for nine hours.

* * *

Thin lenses of silver mist lay over the valley. Uncountable cold-white stars pierced the deep blackness of the mountain night, casting a faint, ghostly radiance across the frosted landscape. Elder stirred and began to awaken. Then looked up with a start. In his slumber he had forgotten about Wolf. His enigmatic companion was seated just a few feet away, watching him. Rustling and grunting, a myopic porcupine was soberly gnawing the base of a nearby tree.

Wolf had been waiting a long time. He wanted to sing again to these mountains. When Elder realized this, he rose and moved stiffly away, demonstrating measured, passive disapproval. Wolf hoped that his new friend's distaste for song would soon soften and transform into active support—even participation.

He started calmly, easily. Resonant, throaty notes rolled down the hillside with the breeze. Slowly tilting his head, Wolf followed with a series of atonal tenor expressions of gradually heightening volume. Eerie, fluid wailings. He was enjoying himself thoroughly and wished to show Elder that singing could be a light, happy experience—fun. As he sang, he opened his eyes just enough to ascertain the other's reaction. Elder was sitting, staring into the distance. He seemed sad. Their bequilled neighbor was paralyzed. A strip of bark dangled from his mouth.

Wolf let his eyelids reclose, his head arch upward until nearly vertical. Ears swept back, his streamlined form was pointing to the stars. His voice played rapidly up through two octaves and burst into full, dramatic song. The mood was no longer light. Swelling in power, his stentorian solo surged throughout the valley and rose to the surrounding peaks. The porcupine defecated in record time.

Each new refrain was as moving as the last. But each was different, having its own distant, mystical quality. Wolf was lost in the song. His senses seemed to have turned inward, as though he were elsewhere. In undulating ululation, he reached for a dynamic, sublime climax. Thereafter his cry began a prolonged descent, evolving into a singularly plaintive, lonely lament.

Breathing heavily, he held his pose as the final notes echoed into the night. Sometime later he became aware that Elder was gently nuzzling him. The old dog was trembling. He had something to confide in Wolf.

SIX

Elder had dreamt while he was sleeping. That in itself was unusual for he did not dream very often. What's more, this dream seemed uncommonly real to him and—especially now—significant. It was of the preceding morning when he and Wolf had met.

Wolf was intensely interested. He had great respect for visions. Sitting bolt upright, he looked acutely alert as he contemplated his companion. Elder was standing, panting lightly. He recalled his dream:

He could see Wolf sitting in the melting snow. And he could see and hear Wolf singing. He felt the same contempt and revulsion in his dream that he had actually experienced. The hawk that had passed over them was there too, flying off toward the horizon.

Then something very strange happened. He could hear a far-off call. It startled him, but not because it had begun suddenly. It was as if he had been unconsciously cognizant of the sound for a long time. As if he had failed to recognize it because it had blended into the natural background. Like the mellow cooing of a mourning dove. Then, there it was.

It was clearly another wolf singing as Wolf had done, answering Wolf. It sounded very, very far away, but there was no mistaking it. Elder was sure of that. It frightened him so much that he was now surprised he hadn't awakened immediately.

Elder was panting more heavily. He was visibly nervous. Wolf blinked, his nostrils dilating as though trying to scent the rest of Elder's story.

The aspect of his dream that disturbed Elder most was not the fact of having heard the remote wolf's reply. It was his own reaction to it. Somehow, some way, it did not revolt him. Absent were the totally negative sensations he had felt upon first hearing Wolf sing. This distant, answering call seemed . . . all right! Even—natural.

Elder was genuinely unnerved. He felt guilty, but

more than that, he was worried about himself. Had he been tainted by some sort of perversion? The old dog picked his way over to a smooth hollow and, after circling three times, lay down. He nested his head between forepaws; his face wore a very uncomfortable expression. Wolf's eyes were aglow. He knew that much more was on Elder's mind. He walked to the old one's side and waited.

The revitalized porcupine, his nose dangerously close to the ground, was still scurrying along strenuously. He was now a quarter of a mile away.

Elder had relived his dream a dozen times while listening to Wolf sing that night. Each time the same fears had haunted him, and his dilemma loomed larger. All the more now because he could not even bring himself honestly to object to Wolf's song. Although he knew that it was evil, this time he had not reflexively rejected it. Wolf was no malevolent fiend. He had been respectful of and helpful to Elder. He seemed sincere, even inspired. His sounds were so powerful. And try as he might, Elder could not fail to recognize a certain beauty in them. Indeed, he sensed profound meaning.

His dream had released something in Elder, had dispelled some blinding, lifelong inhibition. But his sudden freedom left him as yet unable and afraid to make judgments, to resolve his inner conflicts. An owl oo-ooed in the forest below.

Wolf sat down and cocked his head. Elder's eyes

peered sideways to meet the gaze of his friend, and, with new confidence, he continued his confession.

As I thought of these things tonight during your song, I remembered another dream. One I had long ago—when I was a puppy. I guess that I had come to think of it as a sort of foolish nightmare and forced it out of my mind. But my dream tonight brought it back—every detail.

Wolf shifted his feet restlessly, imploring the other to go on. Elder glanced back over his shoulder, then up along the skyline. A thin sickle moon was rising in the east. Ears slightly to the rear, he began panting again—lowly but audibly.

I dreamt of a hunting trip. There was a pack of wolves much like my own family group, although somewhat larger. They were filing through sagebrush into the wind. It was very cold. Suddenly they stopped and milled around in great excitement. They apparently had scented some prey just over a rise in front of them. Then they divided into two columns and moved upslope in different directions.

Oo-oo! Oo-oo! The owl was closer. Wolf was as still as stone.

There must have been a sentry posted above them who gave the alarm because very soon a herd of running animals broke onto the ridge and raced down it away from the wolves. The hunters started to give chase, but it was hopeless. The others were too fast.

They looked a lot like antelope, 'though I couldn't see them very well. But I distinctly remember a large trailing buck. He paused to look back at the wolves and was silhouetted against the sky. I could see clearly that he was a pronghorn, but he had four horns instead of two! That was the only unreal part of the dream—those mythical antelope. Except for the singing.

Wolf blinked again and snorted, fluffing the ruff that framed his face. Elder took a deep breath.

After the pronghorns—whatever you want to call them—were out of sight, the wolves regathered on the ridge and seemed to feel like resting for a while. Some were sniffing tracks; others just stood around or sat down. Then, with my crazy puppy's imagination, I saw and heard several of them start yowling like coyotes.

Wolf lowered his head a little and leaned slightly forward.

Singing you would say. Pretty soon the whole perverted gang was singing shamelessly!

Elder looked away, feeling truly embarrassed—and not a little disgusted by his own thoughtlessness. Almost apologetically, he went on.

They did appear to be relaxed and happy—enjoying themselves. A couple of large puppies who had been rolling on the ground jumped up and tried singing too. It seemed like fun. I felt a sudden urge to join in. That's when I first became conscious of myself in the dream, and I woke up to find myself imitating them.

But not for long. My mother grabbed me by the scruff of the neck and shook me until I was sick. She told me that no whelp of hers would ever experiment with such a disgusting, wicked practice. And I didn't. I was too afraid even to tell her about my dream. I realized that the singing of my dream was merely misguided fancy—part of a puppy's nightmare like the four-horned antelope. I tried to forget it. I had forgotten it—until tonight.

A shadow in the pale moonlight glided over Wolf and Elder. Oo-oo! Oo-oo!

The two wolves felt a strong bond. For a long time they watched each other. Elder's panting gradually subsided. At last he rose and stretched, then sat on his haunches. Wolf stood up.

Do you see, Elder? Do you see?

SEVEN

Elder conveyed mild irritation. He didn't know how Wolf would interpret his dreams. He wasn't sure that he wanted to know. And his pride was chafed by the implication that he couldn't comprehend the significance of his own thoughts. But there was no pedanticism in Wolf. Elder knew that he could neither misconstrue nor ignore the other's honest zeal. The old wolf finally acknowledged that his dreams meant no more than Wolf's visions of Dirus and the supposed past, that uncontrolled imagination could conjure up all sorts of fantasies, pleasant and distasteful.

But, Elder, most of my visits with Dirus have not been dreams. He has come to me when I've been awake—fully conscious. Well, almost fully conscious.

Fanciful reverie then, nothing more. How can you seriously believe that you have seen into the past?

Dirus assured me of that. And it was very real. How can you be so sure that you have not? Don't you consider it a strange coincidence that we have both seen wolves singing as though it were natural for them to do so? Have you ever dreamt of wolves flying, or living underwater like trout? How do you explain your dream tonight of hearing another wolf answering my song? You're never actually heard that.

No, but you had told me of your visions, and I had heard you calling. Those experiences apparently infected my mind sufficiently to cause the dream. And, at least subconsciously, I must've remembered my nightmare as a puppy.

There, you see! How could you have dreamt of wolves singing when you were a puppy? You certainly hadn't been exposed to song then. You must have been born with a memory of the past!

Elder rose and began pacing, pausing occasionally to urinate. His reply was more emphatic than before—and a little desperate. He was counting on it.

Nonsense, Wolf! No more than I was born with a memory of those mythical four-horned antelope. Pure imagination!

Wolf could barely contain himself and hopped over to interrupt the other's meandering.

But you were! Those four-horned antelope were not creations of imagination. I have seen them myself. And Dirus told me that they once roamed all across the prairie. They lived in the past just as wolves sang in the past, and that is where you saw them. There was nothing unreal in that dream.

The scent of a mountain lion patrolling the crags above wafted down to them. Elder stared blankly at his friend. Wolf pressed his advantage.

You told me shortly after we met that you had heard other puppies trying to sing. That you had even helped to suppress one. Isn't it possible that they too had dreamt of their ancestors? You simply cannot dismiss all of this as coincidental imagination. That is the way it really was: wolves expressing themselves in their own way. That is the way it should be again. You must believe me. I want you to help me.

Elder looked away. He scanned the fog-shrouded valley below, following it upstream toward the snow-capped divide. Searching.

A chilling scream from the cougar sliced through the night. Both wolves stood motionless, silently testing the air. At length Elder refocused on Wolf.

What do you propose to do?

Elder sat, and now it was Wolf who seemed ill at ease. Albeit encouraged by what he sensed to be a major change in Elder's attitude, he wished that the depth of his own convictions was matched by the certainty of his plans. He stopped in front of his comrade.

Elder, if you would sing with me, together we could show others—set an example that others might be inspired to follow. Like the two wolves in your dream. That might've been an omen, a prophecy. Maybe we could attract others to join us.

Elder sighed and looked up at the moon. While he lacked Wolf's faith in visions of the past he drew on a lifetime's refinement of common sense. Very much aware of his tacit concessions during their earlier exchanges, Elder had no qualms about being blunt.

That will never work, Wolf. Never! You'll never transform your dreams into reality by trying to convert and recruit adult wolves.

I learned. I learned how satisfying and how good singing can be. It is uplifting. It's a natural joy! And you yourself seem to have become at least tolerant of the idea.

You are . . . different. But I can never learn to sing. The feeling that it is wrong and debasing is just too strong. I may be sympathetic to your faith, and I may give some credence to your beliefs. I may even help you. But I could never bring myself to sing—even if I were still physically able to do so, which I doubt. I suspect that it is an ability which must be developed through practice when one is young.

Wolf started walking away but soon turned back. Elder watched him, feeling superior self-confidence for the first time in his company.

Elder, the ability and predisposition to sing must live within wolves. It's in their makeup.

Perhaps so, but your time is short—too short to be wasted inefficiently. The hostility of adult wolves to what they consider to be disgusting yowling is too great, too universal. You won't make much progress trying to enlighten them.

Wolf felt like singing until his lungs burst, or running as fast as he could for miles. He shook his head from side to side. His greatest frustration was in knowing that Elder was right. He himself had learned that. Lingering soreness in his haunch reminded him of his lesson. And he had not forgotten the young dog for whose severe punishment he felt responsible. He trotted off in a wide circle, marking five boulders and a helpless tree. Elder waited for a few minutes.

Wolf, you presume to tell me of the profound meaning of my dreams, yet you seem to have overlooked or forgotten a much simpler message. It may be too obvious.

Wolf glanced skeptically over at Elder, who was scratching himself.

Namely that . . .

Elder paused for a particularly vigorous raking behind his ear, intentionally delaying his analysis. When he reopened his eyes, he fixed Wolf with an intense gaze.

. . . that puppies offer you the only means of

returning song to our kind. If they are born with a memory of song as you insist—and as they must be if singing is truly natural and good for wolves—then you must nourish that instinct while they are still receptive. Before it is shaken out of them. I believe that this strategy could work.

Wolf pondered the suggestion a moment and walked slowly over to his not-so-dense mentor.

I had thought of that, but I don't see how I can gain access to puppies. They're always protected in family groups. I shall have no opportunity to teach them. Even if I should, they would be punished and I would be driven off. Unless . . .

Wolf could feel Elder smiling.

But it would take so long! Where shall I find a mate? I'm no longer welcome in my home territory. And my mate would have to cooperate in teaching the puppies.

It's your surest way. Probably the only way. Use what you've learned. You will be naturally dominant in your own family. And if racial memory is in the puppies, if the spirit lives, then they shall learn. In one year there will be half a dozen of you . . . if you survive. When the young ones mature, they will follow your lead. There could be an endless chain reaction.

Wolf began panting. One eyelid twitched in a nervous spasm. He was very excited—and very frightened. Elder continued.

Not long ago I spent much time trailing a pack of nine wolves in a broad valley beyond the high divide—about three days toward the evening sun. There was a young bitch trailing them as well—in a sort of marginal status. Not accepted, but tolerated at a distance. She hadn't yet whelped her first litter.

Will you show me the way?

No. I would only complicate matters. The valley has three lakes below small glaciers in its headwater basins. You'll find it.

I may be gone for a long time, Elder. Will you be strong enough to hunt?

Our feast of yesterday is renewing my strength already. And that elk will feed me for weeks. I shall be all right. You had better be on your way. She has a light gray stripe down the middle of her face.

Wolf looked deeply into Elder's warm, yellow-gray eyes. Their tails wagging gently, the two wolves touched noses. Then Wolf turned and trotted down the hillside. Elder watched him disappear into the shadows—on a straight line toward the distant peaks. Dawn was coming to the eastern sky. Gathering clouds would dramatize the sunrise.

EIGHT

Quilts of velvet vapor clung to the valley floor. Wolf paused to chart his course through the sea of supercooled mist. He spied a rocky prominence on the far side; a great gray owl perched on a ridge, looking to the west. Then he plunged into a nebulous world of cloud. As a shadow he drifted over the frosted field. Chilling fog streamed past his head and shoulders, crystallizing on his whiskers. Floating veils mingled with images of huddled willows and solitary lodgepole pines. Each blade and needle was sheathed in delicate ice.

Approaching the stream, Wolf felt the presence of Shiras moose. He thought that he perceived a dark shape hulking in the gloom. It was indistinct, then gone. An ephemeral creature, perhaps imagined. Diffuse forms of wolves appeared and vanished. They left no scent. There was a strange feeling of immeasurable slowness—of time barely moving. Wolf watched the silent mists shifting and swirling in slow motion over the pond's glazed surface. He had a sensation of wanting to shiver, but his body would not respond.

A quality of unreality pervaded all, rising and falling through Wolf's consciousness. A slow breathing of a silent wind. An untouchable dimension almost within reach of his senses. He recognized impressions that brought back in instantaneous mélange all that he associated with Dirus. He called for Dirus. His guidance now would be reassuring and bolstering. But Wolf knew that this time Dirus was not there. And yet he felt an unmistakable presence, an inexplicable essence, living and close.

For just a moment the rising sun broke through waves of low gray clouds flowing over the mountains and illuminated the valley in orange bronze. Its semi-translucent cloak of fog both reflected and absorbed the dawn's brilliance, becoming infused with an almost blinding glow. An aura of vibrant, blazing iridescence. The hovering mists seemed incandescent—in their own way, alive. Cold, calm fire. Then as the sun was again concealed, the brightness faded—and with it ebbed Wolf's special feeling of union with time.

He leapt the stream at a place where its channel ran narrow and deep. Over to the base of the ridge and up, out of the mist. He climbed rapidly and straight. Jumping brush and boulders, he angled up the steep slope toward the ridge's higher reaches and passed beneath the great gray owl where it merged into the mountain. A cold wind fluttered peach-gold aspen. Traces of Gulo's forceful odor: the wolverine. On toward timberline.

How would it be—teaching puppies? How would they react? Could generations of repression and condemnation permeate the mind, still emotion, blind the senses? Could natural love of beauty—of free voice—survive, prevail? Appeal to soul, succeed? It seemed to Wolf that he must know how violence had been done in order surely to undo it.

Warmer air. He was ahead of the cold and clouds. Behind, the rolling blanket pressed relentlessly over the foothills and lower ridges, banking in toward the high range. Wolf's hackles sprang up as he passed through a vestige of grizzly scent. Several large, naked rocks had been uprooted, their lichen-covered faces down. One lay next to a large mound of fresh earth where the bear had excavated a marmot the day before.

When he topped the ridge, Wolf bore to the left

and moved gradually upward along its crest. Ten thousand feet above sea level he entered a towering stand of green-black Engelmann spruce. Sloping branches swayed gently in the unsettled air, testing their strength for an anticipated burden of snow. Trotting through their shadows, Wolf wondered how long it had taken to destroy song.

Quack-like cries interplayed with almost hysterical hootings as a group of gray jays glided from tree to tree. Bosses of rust-brown rock loomed ahead like a congregation of colossal tortoises. Wolf skirted the clearing and left them to their unending deliberations. On the far side the slope eased down into a shallow dip beyond which shorter, bushier spruce thinned and yielded to rocky tundra on the mountain above. What could have motivated Rufus? Had he imposed solely his own will? Had he gone mad?

A cold breeze ruffled Wolf's fur as he crossed the saddle. Clouds were beginning to cluster around peaks of the high divide to the southwest. Rising above timberline, the ridge Wolf was following tapered to a jagged spine of vertical slabs. A long, curved bank of drifted snow formed a fringing shoulder on the right. He hesitated. There, he would traverse the left side of the mountain beneath its near summit, moving up toward the crest of the range beyond. A narrow pass promised access to the western slope of the divide.

Wolf picked his way cautiously across the steep

incline. The flow of damp, chilling air was steady now. It smelled like snow. Wolf looked back along the ridge and into the valley from which he had come—and where Elder was.

The encroaching tide of cloud seemed to be self-multiplying, thickening even as Wolf beheld it. Its upper layers coursed across the sky above him, surging in silent turbulence to envelop the mountaintops. Underneath advanced a billowing wall of white gray, enshrouding the shoulders of the valley walls, masking the valley itself. The elk meadow was hidden, then the beaver dams. And the slopes beyond—the site of their feast. Although Elder could not possibly see him, Wolf knew that his friend was watching.

Elder lay curled where he had slept the day before. The turn to colder weather bothered him not at all. He was cozy and comfortable. He felt physically well—better than in a very long time. But his mind was with Wolf. He had actually wanted to go along. He grew uneasy as the heavy overcast obscured the last of the high peaks. He jerked his right hind leg and nuzzled it vigorously to relieve a cramp in the haunch.

Wolf was several hundred yards from the divide when the air bloomed into snow. Tiny, stinging granules at first—a sweeping white sandstorm. The mountainside was covered in minutes. Because of lowering clouds Wolf had barely been able to fix the pass he sought before the snow. Now he could see virtually nothing. Blurred images of his own feet, the protected faces of rocks—all else was awash in white. And as the snow transformed into softer, larger flakes, the whiteness became almost total.

Accelerating as it funneled into the col above, the wind buffeted Wolf from the left and rear. Maintaining his equilibrium became difficult even when stationary. He chose to use his tail for protection, nestling it down between his back legs, but thereby sacrificed its stabilizing potential as a rudder. His head was turned down, away from the gale-driven snow. Ears back, left eye closed, right eye squinting, he probed and tested with his forepaws. And he inched his way forward and upward over the snow-covered talus.

To keep from losing his balance and being blown repeatedly against the rocks, Wolf had to lean outward. But then when he did slip, as often as not he tumbled downslope in a bruising, flailing tangle and had to rely on protruding boulders to arrest his descent. Righting himself after a particularly jolting fall, he planted splaying feet with defiant determination and shook very carefully. It was becoming painfully obvious that he had not selected the most favorable time for crossing the Great Divide.

Facing away from the wind, his eyes searched the tempestuous whiteness through the narrowest of slits. As if incurably nearsighted, he stretched his neck forward in the hope of resolving some recognizable shape. The pass must lie in that direction. He had no idea how much progress he had made toward it. Perhaps he should wedge himself among the rocks, balled up to wait for the storm to subside. But how long would that be? How deep would the drifts become? No. Go on now.

Wolf was developing an unreasoned belief, a faith, that he was in no real danger, that he could not fall victim to the natural elements of his world. That only time stood between him and his goals—if his commitment were sufficiently strong. He snorted, lowered his head, and forged onward with renewed resolve.

Step by step, rock by rock, cautiously forward and upward. There was no use in looking up—wind and snow swirled into his eyes. He might as well have been blind. He stared at his paws, transferring weight gradually with each new footfall. Although pressed against his head, his soft-furred ears had become numb with cold and had lost to the wind their sensitivity for sound. Reeeee! It raged, seeming stronger. Was he nearing the top? The snow was actually streaming upward. Several inches had already accumulated, but most had been driven into long, narrow drifts trailing upslope in the lee of rocks.

Snow from the sky, snow from the ground: mixed

by the wind in a continuum of white. Wolf was not aware that he had been engulfed by clouds. In their upper levels they emitted the white light of the sun itself. This brilliance radiated in all directions, reflecting from each snowflake and cloud crystal. An unending white flash. Wolf could not withstand its piercing, painful intensity. He stopped and closed his eyes tightly, turning his lowered head slowly from side to side. Then again he felt his way forward.

A smoother surface. No more rocks. He had crossed the talus and stood on snow-swept tundra. Wolf sighed, flinching at the memory of countless collisions with boulders. He peeked ahead—but just for an instant. White! Like coming out of a cave.

With sudden energy he sprang forward and began trotting diagonally upslope. And he quickly learned that negotiating the smooth but steep incline of tundra was even more treacherous than crossing the rocks. His feet skied from under him, and he began rolling downhill like a log. Now he hoped that he would crash into a boulder at least once more.

With desperate effort he flipped himself onto his stomach, his head pointing uphill. Raking his hind feet into the snow in an erratic running motion, he curled his outstretched forepaws and hooked his claws like talons into the frozen ground. After a short slide in this position he slowed and stopped. His frustration was rising into anger. He would reach that pass or die trying. And Wolf rested and thought about that for a while.

Had he been foolish in persisting along the most direct route to the divide? If so, his luck had certainly not been of the best. Or was he in some way again being tested, his will challenged? How? Why? He was not trying to establish dominance over the mountain. He wanted only to get on with his work, his life. Wolf rose.

Crouching so low that his ribs brushed the ground, he clawed and pushed and pulled himself back up the slope. Past the place from which he had just fallen. His own scent was the first his nose had credited since the onset of the storm. The solar white glare was somewhat dimmer, so occasionally he opened his eyes in a fluttering squint to peer ahead. But still he could discern nothing to give him a bearing. Dimensionless albescence. He knew only that he was moving up, opposite to the direction of falling. And now the wind was behind him, helping.

Soon the grade became more gentle. As it flattened, the gale accelerated, rising in pitch. Wolf could no longer hold his crouch. To his surprise, he was walking, then trotting in the air stream. He strained to see where he was going with such unexpected rapidity. The view remained wholly white. But it was now focused in almost hypnotic perspective. Myriad snowflakes streaking together in the screaming jet, converging as to the neck of an invisible funnel. Confluent lines of white ice. An imploding universe.

The compelling current drove Wolf ever faster—much faster than he felt safe in traveling with zero visibility. He was galloping up the gentle rise—but trying to slow down. Abruptly the slope crested. Wolf was propelled over the top and found himself hurtling downhill into deepening drifts. The pass! He had breached the divide.

Thrusting stiffened forelegs into the snow, he braked and halted, sitting hard on his hindquarters. Wolf sat motionless, momentarily bewildered. He could listen and look again. Ears erect, eyes agape, he beheld his surroundings.

The change was stunning. Quiescence. The wind had gone. He was in clouds, but they had lost their blinding brilliance. Small snowflakes were falling thickly and steadily. Now gently, quietly. Softly sifting in silent breath from the sky. Time seemed to be slowing again, barely flowing—if at all. Wolf could see, but there was no sound, no scent. Strange feelings. Sensations of—suspension. Incalculable distance.

Behind him on the right he perceived a gray, angular form. A huge overhanging monolith above a sheltered hollow. Motion! Something moved there. A round dark patch. Wolf bounded eagerly toward it with exaggerated leaps through the snowbank. Not solid color—sort of speckled brown. It ran. Rock ptarmigan! Still partially clothed in summer plumage. Pacing like a prairie chicken, the bird crossed in front of Wolf and darted downhill on top of the snow. He gave chase. Although slogging through the drifts was frustratingly slow, he gained steadily and was about to make a final lunge when his quarry took wing. Silent wings.

Wolf vaulted into the snow-filled air, vainly attempting to bat the ptarmigan down. The bird vanished in whiteness. He glanced down just in time to see that he was landing near the edge of a high, rocky bluff. As he was about to touch he plunged his feet to the ground like pistons, springing himself back away from the precipice.

He fell on his side and rolled upright. Staring out from the cliff, he noticed that the snowfall was abating. He thought that he could begin to see some shadows, vague shapes. Perhaps the upper parts of trees below showing through the snow. There—he was certain. Two diffuse images were moving. Ptarmigan flying? No. And as if he were gliding to them through the fringes of a fog, by degrees they enlarged, took on form and color, and came into focus.

Boom. Boom. Boom! BOOM! His heart. The only sound. Then the low, threatening growl. Before him in the sky stood a very large, reddish brown wolf. A mature dog with straight tail cocked obliquely upward in the position of challenge. Rufus!

NINE

Wolf sat immobilized. The tension in his muscles was almost beyond control. Reflexive energy set to explode into action: self-defense and counter-challenge. But only his pulsing nostrils and searching eyes gave animation to his rigid form. For he had grasped immediately that he was not a physical part of the vision he beheld. With an expression blending intense interest and innocent confidence, Wolf watched in pure wonder.

Rufus' assertions of dominance were directed toward a smaller wolf in the left of Wolf's view. A younger gray dog, cowering and backing away. With tail curled down, ears back, and teeth bared, his body was hunched in an arch of submission. As Rufus sprang toward him, the young dog rolled over on his back and folded his paws. But still he showed his teeth. He had given in quickly. He had had no choice. But he didn't like it.

Again in the posture of challenge and dominance, Rufus glowered down at his conquest. The big brownish wolf was uncommonly large and powerfully built. Even larger than he himself, Wolf judged. Imposing. Exuding strength. But even as his coat was strongly pigmented, Rufus' eyes were very pale, lacking depth of color. Like dead grass.

Stop cringing, Cur, and stand up!

The young dog's lips receded further and he snarled nervously—but with pluck. Leave me alone. I don't want to fight you. That would be pointless. I yield. Can't you see that?

Then stand up, Cur. Show some self-respect. Stand up like a wolf! And Rufus moved back a few steps, assuming a pose designed to convey contempt.

The other disliked having been forced to acknowledge inferiority so abjectly—and so unnecessarily. But he was even more annoyed by being insulted for it. He gathered his feet under him, rose slowly, and shook. At length he turned cautiously toward Rufus. The instant their eyes met the larger wolf lunged and seized the gray dog's neck in his jaws.

This took the young wolf completely by surprise. In view of what had already happened he had no reason to expect more physical abuse. It was an act of brutish intimidation and it frightened him. At first he tried to pull away, but the jaws tightened their clench to induce pain. He stopped struggling. What do you want of me? I'll go elsewhere if you wish.

Rufus jerked his head, and violently hurled his captive to the ground among green grass and flowers.

It was spring at the time and place of this scene. Wolf stared with absolute concentration, unaware of whether or not he was breathing. The snow fell with unnatural slowness. He was looking beyond it. And he could hear without listening.

I want you to accept me as your superior and leader.

But your size and strength and aggressiveness make it natural for you to be dominant over me. I relented immediately in the manner of our kind. My signals couldn't have been more obvious. The young dog arranged himself more comfortably in the grass and gazed into the distance. He avoided Rufus, who once again took the initiative.

I do not admire exhibitions of cowardice. Nor do I care one whit for the ritualistic niceties of social interaction—nor for a good many other traditional stupidities. Wastes of time without purpose perpetuated by so-called lovers of the natural way. Self-rationalizing weaklings! I ask for . . . I *demand* your allegiance. Rufus' stance was defiant. He challenged the other to look at him, but he would not.

The smaller wolf was afraid to respond. Or to move. Finally gathering courage, he looked skyward. I do not understand you. I did not subordinate myself to you out of cowardice. It was natural for me to do so, if you will pardon that. I have learned to behave thus in such circumstances so as to preserve harmony. It seems to me that it is a good way, a way of acknowledging differences in physical and personality traits without losing face on either side. What is the point of trying to stare down a larger, more aggressive wolf? I was taught that this is one of the important means by which we prevent unnecessary and potentially harmful conflicts among ourselves.

He shuddered slightly as Rufus advanced a few steps to confront him. He could feel the big wolf's wrathful eyes. Panting, he continued.

As to my allegiance, I shall be willing to join you—and to follow you. So long as it is to our mutual advantage. And I am sure that it will be to mine. You must have a great deal more experience and skill in hunting than I do. Is this your territory? Are you the leader of a group? I'm passing through this area and haven't yet met any other wolves.

Where are *you* from, Cur? Rufus sat down, still glaring.

My home pack lives in the foothills along the edge of the plains. But there are many adults. I was not permitted to stay. I . . .

You were whelped in the spring before last?

Yes. Early. There was much snow. Three of my littermates died. Where is your pack?

I have no pack.

But why? You are in your prime. And exceptionally strong.

I had trouble with them. I chose to leave.

What sort of trouble? Rufus did not reply for a long time.

I had to discipline a subordinate. The others reacted negatively. They took his part and ganged up on me. I couldn't handle them all at once, so I left. I'd be surprised if they're still functioning. Sniveling cowards! I could have dealt with them individually—even in pairs. Rufus was clearly becoming angrier as he thought about it.

The younger wolf was suddenly alarmed. He shifted his legs. But curiosity overcame his apprehension. Why should they have driven you off? How could they bring themselves to do that if you were their leader?

I *was* their leader! It was mutiny. Born of jealousy. Their pretext was that I was too harsh. I wasn't permissive enough for them. Anyway, that dog I killed was a useless loafer.

The gray wolf was incredulous. Thunderstruck. Do you mean that you actually killed one of your own group?!

I tore out his throat.

TEN

Reverberations of a deep rumbling filled Wolf's ears. A growl from the abyss of his being. Yet he made not a sound. He remained utterly still. Not in awe—in horror.

The young wolf was on his feet. Why? Why??!

Rufus bristled. Because he was of an inferior strain—retarded. A throwback like so many of that type. He persisted in imitating coyotes, yowling all the time. I had warned him. Repeatedly. But he ignored me. He tried to convince the others that it was his right, his freedom. That I was in error. Well, now he has absolute and eternal freedom. Besides, he interrupted my rest. I silenced him for good.

With this Rufus turned and trotted over to urinate on a sapling pine. Then he looked back at his trembling acquaintance. You seem sickly. Have you fed lately?

In his disbelief the gray dog had forgotten himself and was watching Rufus. After a lengthy pause he looked down. Not well. A few days ago I found an old deer carcass, a cougar kill. There wasn't much left, and that was rotten.

Join me now and hunt. When you've eaten we'll get on with our mission.

What mission?

Later. Let's go. And Rufus moved off toward a scattered stand of giant ponderosas.

A sudden wave of wind churned the curtain of snow into shifting eddies. But they calmed as quickly as they had formed. Wolf looked on.

The young gray wolf ran his tongue along his upper lips from one side of his mouth to the other. Stretching out to enjoy the cool shade, he rested his head on long, smooth pine needles. He didn't know how Rufus had detected the scentless fawn in the high grass, but his stomach was full. He was satisfied, if somewhat logy, and he appreciated having been allowed to feed first. He raised his head lazily as Rufus approached.

The other was still munching something, crunching a bit of bone. A few grayish, blood-spattered feathers stuck to his ruff.

What are you eating?

Great horned owl. A young one.

Do you like owls? I mean—as food?

Rufus snarled. No. I detest everything about owls! Look, don't plan on a long rest. We've some traveling to do.

Where?

Two valleys over.

The young dog eased up on his elbows with exaggerated effort. Why? What's the rush?

That is my intention, Cur. Is that enough?

A pause. Yes. But can't you elaborate?

We must get on with my work. There's no time to fritter away loafing. Rufus was emphatic and wore a very serious expression.

Reluctantly the smaller wolf stood up and shook. What's so important? What are we going to do?

What is important is the survival of wolves! I have committed myself to that end above all else. And if you truly care for the future of your own kind, you will also.

His young companion was relieved by this refreshing appeal to reason, but he didn't follow the reasoning. What do you mean? You certainly seem capable of surviving.

I mean the survival of wolves as a race—and their strengthening in the process.

The gray wolf was confused. Rufus pushed toward his point. Are there more or less wolves in your home territory than there used to be?

The other hesitated. Well, less. My former home pack is smaller than it once was and there are fewer wolves overall. Neighboring packs have been declining. When I left one was down to only four adults and hadn't been successful in rearing puppies for three seasons.

Why?

Prey was very scarce. My mother wasn't able to get enough from her portions of the occasional kills to feed half of my brothers and sisters adequately. That's why they were weak and couldn't survive the bad weather. And that's why I was not admitted to the pack. None of the young wolves are now. And no new wolves are accepted from outside. They're trying to reduce the number of mature wolves so that the size of the pack will be better suited to the food supply. Some have even suggested migrating to a different area. But what are you getting at? Why are you so . . .

My name is *Rufus!*

Very well . . . Rufus. That's fitting. I am Gray. I do not like the name Cur. And the young dog looked away nervously, sensing the other's irritation. Rufus began slowly circling Gray, watching him closely.

Why has your pack been having such a hard time? Are they weak? Are they poor hunters? Rufus seemed distinctly unsympathetic and yet purposeful in his questioning.

That's difficult for me to judge. I have never known it to be different. According to some of the old wolves, the climate was less severe and the game more plentiful in the time of our ancient ancestors. Perhaps that's part of it. I . . .

Have you ever hunted in the mountains? In the mountain valleys? Rufus' pupils appeared to shrink as he became more eager.

Gray was surprised. Why, no. There would be no point in that. Most of them are full of ice and contain little or no prey.

Has it always been this way?

I don't know—I guess not. The older wolves believe that the ice has been creeping farther down every season, that the high valleys used to be open and good hunting territory. And that the winters are longer and more severe than in the old days, the summers shorter and less mild.

That is the truth! The great streams of ice have been a growing menace for uncounted seasons—for generations of wolves beyond memory. Packs used to live and hunt in every mountain valley. Deer, elk, and moose were abundant. And sheep in the high country. They prospered there. Many migrated to the lowlands in winter, making hunting much easier for us. Now few can find even summer range above the foothills. Their numbers have declined drastically.

And not just here. The results of these changes can be seen everywhere—even at great distances across the plains beyond your comprehension. Especially in the direction of long winter darkness. In other places there is much rain, floods, huge lakes where animals of the flat country formerly thrived. This is all part of the greatest hardship and challenge wolves have ever faced. The future is in peril!

Rufus had stopped to face Gray and was trembling with enthusiasm. The younger wolf sat down slowly. He was shaken.

Is it really true? How can you be so certain about all these things?

Information has been passed on. I know. Believe me. And Rufus advanced a few steps.

That's frightening. Gray looked down at a pine cone. What do you mean it's only *part* of our challenge?

Aha! Now you've come to the key. We are equal to this and can overcome it—if we have the will. But we must be dedicated. We must recommit ourselves to the old virtues of strength and single-mindedness.

We cannot afford disunity. Nor any debilitating frivolities.

I'm not sure I understand.

You should. You saw three littermates die. Wolves can no longer afford the inefficiency of individuality. Our strength and survival are overriding—far more important than territorial or group prerogatives. The perpetuation of our kind requires aggressive leadership and unity. We must suppress and eliminate weakness and division. And those who promote or even condone them.

Rufus looked to the clouds, disdainfully ignoring three noisy crows that crossed his view. His expression was detached, almost spiritual. Gray was watching him again, now with a mixture of heightened curiosity and —for the first time—admiration.

We must reassume our rightful status, taking pride in our power and wolfliness. Uncompromising in our rejection of diluting and debasing elements. Let all other kinds imitate us. Let us stand above them. He turned again to his young companion. Rufus' eyes were full and focused. They shone with disarming intensity.

Let coyotes chase mice and cry to the moon. Our contempt for such acts shall symbolize our resolve to reassert our purity and preeminence. Let wolves not indulge in futility. Let us not abide unwolfliness.

Rufus stood, solid and massive. Seeming larger than life. His deep chest was heaving. Panting lightly,

Gray closed his eyes for a moment. Now he knew. But he was unsure what to believe. Was Rufus motivated primarily by concern for the welfare of wolves, or was he merely rationalizing his own appetite for power? Was the widespread practice of singing—which Gray himself had learned, but to which he dare not refer—truly a weakening, demeaning mimicry of lower animals? Or did this argument simply express a personal dislike of Rufus, manifest some warp in the big wolf's makeup?

Abruptly Rufus turned away and broke into an easy but determined lope. Let's get busy!

What do you have in mind?

You'll learn that on the way. And, despite his reservations, the young dog went along. A blue grouse flushed at the last minute, flapping noisily and startling Gray. In its frantic flight the heavy bird rolled crazily and nearly collided with a tree.

Snowflakes filled the air before Wolf. He stared with the same wide eyes and still had not moved. There was an undetectably light breeze. Instead of blowing, it seemed to be slowly sucking, almost audibly. But without direction.

In an instant, Rufus and Gray were trotting toward willows near the center of a wide, sage-rimmed valley. A new setting.

We shall shortly meet a lone dog wolf working

along the far side of the floodplain. Follow my instructions and it will be quick and simple. Although Rufus' order seemed ominous, his manner was casual.

There. The dog scented them. He stood alert, nose tilted up, searching the air. Tense. Average size. Gray and cream. And thin.

We shall approach him directly but separately, angling from each side. Once close, at my signal you feint an attack. Then I'll take over.

So it was. The stranger was guarded but not alarmed. Rufus walked up from the right, Gray from the left. All three were rigid. The atmosphere was uncertain. As if ready to spark.

Move! And from a few feet Gray obediently shouldered forward, drawing a defensive turn. At the instant the stranger was diverted, Rufus crushed him from the other side. Iron-strong jaws closed through loose-furred throat skin. Braking and rearing, Rufus muscled his victim upward and, with a savage twist, spun him across his shoulders like a heavy goose. The neck vertebrae spiraled and severed.

Gray ran off. In green aspens half a mile away he vomited. Ultimately the needs of his mouth and stomach drove him back to the stream. Rufus was waiting. Sitting indifferently. After a furtive glance, the younger dog lowered his head and drank slowly and delicately, eyes closed. As full as was comfortable, he paused and looked toward the horizon.

Rufus rose and stretched. Simple, wasn't it?

Simple? Yes, very simple. But for what possible reason?

That dog's mate has a new litter of puppies. And now no help in feeding and rearing them. We shall fill the gap. You as mate-father. I as hunter-provider. Sort of—adopted uncle. And teacher. Leader! The bitch shall have no choice.

I cannot bring myself to do that. You be the father. It's your idea. I think I'll just leave.

You shall stay and play your part. I will not waste my time in the role of mate and parent. And Rufus marked a beaver-gnawed aspen stump, which faded in a screen of snow.

ELEVEN

Wolf was appalled. Dirus had not exaggerated. All that was happening was so full of meaning for him, so disturbing, that for a moment he felt oversaturated, in need of distraction. He became conscious of his eyes; they had been relaxed—looking to infinity. As he pulled his head back he shortened his focus to watch the floating flakes of snow. They appeared to be drifting down with imperceptible slowness. He wondered if he might be seeing the same crystals in suspension, if their apparent motion were imagined, assumed by his senses. In reality the episodes Wolf perceived must have spanned considerable time. But he had no awareness of it. He did not blink. Then again his vision lengthened.

Darkness! Thick, vivid darkness. Forms shifting languidly as in semicongealed black gelatin. A flash of lightning. Wolves! Many, many wolves. Milling in unsettled assembly. The scene came closer, enlarging. Apparent now was the almost constant play of static discharge in a distant thunderhead. It illuminated the gathering with faint psychedelic flickering, exaggerating the subtlest movements.

Another brilliant flash. This one repeating four times in less than a second. Almost all are dogs. Forty, fifty? And all young—large. An outsize brownish wolf was pulling himself to the top of a pedestal rock in their midst. The restlessness stilled. All knew Rufus and turned to face him. All stood rigidly braced with straightened tails pointing diagonally upward as if in a stance of challenge. And in silent unison they pledged their lives to the purity, strength, and unity of wolves. Then, as sepulchral thunder rumbled and rolled across the plains, Rufus began.

As you know this constitutes our final meeting. Your formal training has ended. Tonight is the commencement of our time.

Emotions were extremely high. Nearly every wolf

was bristling and trembling. The excitement was contagious, reinforced by the unusually large size of the group. And given an especially scintillating quality by the dim, oscillating light, the resonating thunder. In Rufus' inner circle were four wolves: three dogs of the first litter he had converted—plus Gray. Gray was slightly smaller than the others. And visibly less enthusiastic. After a calculated pause, Rufus continued.

My work here has been completed. I must move on to our next region. Henceforth you will be on your own, widely dispersed in our mission groups. Rufus commanded total attention. His appearance, his manner, his very presence was spellbinding.

I know that you *shall* succeed. You are all of strong body and character. Even more important, you are of one mind: dedicated to fulfilling our destiny. To achieving a universal greatness for wolves that cannot be diminished in our lifetimes—nor for a thousand generations!

Their leader was gazing into the night sky. All held still. Not a wolf was breathing. Only low tremors of thunder. Then Rufus stepped down. At this signal the others relaxed their poses and began moving excitedly about in the fluttering light.

Many wolves crowded in around Rufus. Some nudged and muzzled him fraternally; others less forward paid homage from a distance through subtle signs acknowledging dominance. Groups of threes and fours were soon departing in different directions. As the remaining numbers thinned, Gray moved to his leader's side.

Rufus, will you be leaving tonight or in the morning? Shall I accompany you?

I'll go over those plans with you privately in a moment. Rufus did not look directly at him.

But before long the big wolf turned and, trotting down the gentle slope with four other wolves, indicated that he would see Gray. This puzzled the younger dog, who had thought that they would meet alone. He was well acquainted with only one of the others, and him he did not like. A tall, rangy wolf who was blindly loyal to Rufus but whom Gray considered to be stupid and sadistically brutal.

Gray eased into a lope and caught up with them as they were crossing a shallow gully. They seemed to have slowed, awaiting him. He bounded into the group and stopped short. Rufus stood sideways, looking straight ahead. The other four immediately surrounded Gray. He spewed out the scent of fear.

What is it?!

Rufus turned. You, Cur, cannot be trusted. You are a potential traitor. Therefore, an enemy. And the reddish wolf feinted a lunge.

Gray knew better, but his reflexes impelled him away to the side. As he swerved he was jolted from behind and plunged into the dust. Gray's fear and pain and shock flowed together during that agonizing instant in which his life was taken.

Lightning revealed a ghastly scene. The rangy dog did not simply kill Gray. He ripped and shredded, exposing bones of body and every limb. Then he proceeded to fracture and splinter some of these.

TWELVE

Another flash whitened the night. It continued—without flickering. Wolf was not conscious of the change, but he had again focused on the immediate sky of snow.

Although he had fed the day before, he felt a hollow, sickening ache in his stomach. Much like the nausea of acute hunger. For the first time in what seemed to be most of a day, Wolf realized an urge to breathe. He inhaled slowly and very deeply, repeating this over and over to relieve his queasiness. He feared that for a long while he would be able to concentrate on little because of the dark scenes to which he had just been witness. His mind had no categories for them; it was incapable of handling them, frustratingly uncomfortable and disordered. In static-electric chaos. How to deal with nightmares known to be real?

Now brightness. Not the white glare of snow and fog, but the blue brilliance of clear midday. Fingers of ice cloud still reached over the crest of the range behind, but no farther. The storm was confined to the eastern side. Below, the western slope displayed itself in the rich verdure and gold of high-country fall. Timbered rocky ridges and broad basins, lakes fed by the remnants of snowfields and glaciers.

Surveying these vistas, Wolf noted that the divide turned toward the evening sun. Its alpine terrain rose in rugged relief, accentuated by etchings of snow fringing the shade of its higher reaches. Remembering Elder's directions, Wolf knew that his journey was yet long. He would be negotiating these mountains for at least two more arcs of the sun. After his punishing ordeal of snow and boulders, he had no inclination, no need to prove himself here. He would move below the snow—through the basins, over lower ridges.

Profoundly troubled, Wolf nonetheless pulled himself up and began walking—rapidly and deliberately. Raw desire now overcame all the rest. His will carried him beyond the past. He shall find his mate. The renewal of his life. His purpose.

Down smooth, rolling tundra he padded. Over parallel stripes of stones descending the intricate carpet of delicate plants. Through a scattered vanguard of heroic trees: solitary and stunted. Breaching low ramparts of massed spruce. A Clark's nutcracker appeared and flew on ahead as if to tease—or lead.

Something immediate seemed wrong. A mild disquiet welled to the surface. It was not Wolf's way to march resolutely past such beauty, oblivious to all the loveliness around him. At the edge of a boulder field he stopped. Closing his eyes and shaking his head, neck, and shoulders, he submerged haunting visions of Rufus' deeds and suppressed countless uncertainties of the future. With a tremulous sigh he blinked and again sensed the world. It was alive!

A fluffy pika peered with black-bead eyes from its cranny among the rocks, regularly emitting a chirring squeak. The button bleat of a stuffed toy. Round ears barely showing, it hunched motionless, a furry cobble—except for its wriggling rabbit nose. Shrill whistles in series announced a lazy gathering of corpulent, sun-basking marmots on boulders below. The soft upslope breeze brought a rich blend of living scents: moist meadow grass in the basin, lake water, the musk of mule deer, a black-footed ferret. Far below in the valley a thin line crossing a pond trailed a beaver purposefully ferrying a mouthful of willow branches to be secured underwater near its lodge.

Glancing to the right, Wolf noticed three white patches against distant rocks. Each seemed to be part of a massive warm-gray form. Half a mile across the slopes stood the trio of arrogantly majestic bighorn rams, their telescopic eyes resolving every detail of Wolf. He watched them with unashamed reverence.

He had never experienced a moment quite like this. A moment of consuming sensual awareness and appreciation following upon the opposite extreme of numbing horror. Pulses of excitement scintillated from his spine in a crescendo of gloriously good feelings. More abruptly than he had halted, he launched himself downhill in an almost reckless, bounding lope. The marmots vanished.

Wolf moved steadily under the afternoon sun. By sunset he was nine miles beyond the beaver pond atop a forested moraine ridge. He interrupted his constant panting to lick his lips. Thirst. Down to the valley. He paused on the bank and gazed thoughtfully at his image. Where was Dirus? He started to crouch and stretch out to drink, but suddenly he dropped himself into the cold, shoulder-high current. It soothed his rock-worn feet. A pair of trumpeter swans paddled noiselessly around a bend and out of sight.

Finally satisfied, he stood for a while in the channel. Water dripped from his muzzle. Faint mists were gathering over the surface of the stream, and through them he viewed rippling reflections of the evolving evening colors: segmented ribbons of flamboyant orange; then vermillion, lavender, and violet fleeting into serene pale gray.

After shaking and rolling in the grass, Wolf sat and simply enjoyed the cool, refreshing dusk. It was a time for singing. As he thought of it, the need grew wildly and became total: physical, emotional, spiritual. Almost beyond his control. But control it he did. He dared not attract attention or risk offending or alarming local wolves. His song could wait—for a while.

Strange rattling yodels echoed up the valley from a vast meadow downstream and mingled with the murmuring music of the rapids. Inimitable calls combining elements of the loon's frenzied cry and the gobble of a tom turkey. They gradually became less frequent, then ceased. The sandhill crane's farewell to the day. And now the fabric of night sounds seemed incomplete and unfinished—flimsy. A symphony without strings. Wolf knew that indeed it was. Oo-oo! Oo-oo! Wolf was galloping westward.

* * *

Another day and another night passed as he moved on, traveling without rest. The weather remained fair: warm in the afternoon, ideally cool under the stars. Near the middle of the third day, the chain of high peaks above turned sharply to the right—again northward. At this bend an immense, densely timbered ridge continued down to the west, at length merging into foothills. Rather than follow this spur away from the mountains, Wolf promptly decided to climb to its highest shoulder.

Struggling breathlessly to the top, he welcomed a fresh northwest breeze and the screen of clouds building overhead. At the crest the airflow approached gale force. He paused and, bracing himself, squinted into the wind, letting its coolness streamline his face and body. He had glimpsed the panorama before him and was postponing the formidable new challenge it posed.

Ascending on the right, this ridge rose into an extravagantly jagged range, a row of monumental teeth towering another two thousand feet toward the sky. Far below the headwaters of a major river coursed down a great yawning canyon. It was exceptionally steep-walled and even wider than it was deep. Parks of green and yellow were strung along the bottom amidst stands of gigantic spruce and fir festooned with hangings of moss. Straight across loomed a single massive mountain draped in aprons of loose rock and crowned by sheer cliffs of pink gray granite.

This valley was so enormous, so distinctive, that Wolf was certain it was not the drainage to which Elder had referred. So he must cross it. Tired now, he worked his way down the incline with care. A mature golden eagle soared on the updraft.

Near the bottom Wolf drank from a cold tributary spring. Then, having forded the main waterway in a shallow riffle, he trotted through head-high grass to the far wall and began his ascent. Bearing to his left, he circumvented the base of the precipitous summit and headed toward the western side of the peak where the slopes were smoother and more agreeable. Doggedly he pushed himself. Past evergreens, aspens, rock slides, and avalanche chutes. Over the rim and across the bare shoulders of the mountain—away from the deep valley and on to the north.

He must have covered at least two miles, perhaps three, when he first caught sight of the next drainage basin. His pulse quickened. So did his pace. He had a special feeling.

It was a broad, shallow valley compared to the last. Narrowing to a deeper ravine in the west, it opened eastward into a huge embayment in the divide. Fed by a threefold cluster of subbasins, the depression resembled the mold of a giant cloverleaf. Wolf could see no lakes or glaciers from his position. But he knew that they were there. Air from the northwest was dropping in temperature, and the sky was now generally overcast.

Excitedly he trotted downhill toward mid-valley below the confluence of the three branches. A tuft-eared lynx watched from atop a nearby boulder, but Wolf ignored the cat. His mind was fully occupied. Could he find the lone bitch Elder had described? If

he did, would she join him? Would her reaction to song be so negative as to preclude their mating and raising puppies? He was both impatient and apprehensive, but nervous energy had displaced his fatigue.

As he descended the lower flanks of the mountain, Wolf instinctively broke into a pattern of search. Instead of a direct traveling course, he zigzagged down the gentler incline in long, sweeping arcs. Nose in maximum play and held close to the ground, his eyes scanned far ahead, back and forth. Pluming straight out behind, his limber tail eased down each time he halted and, ears erect, held his panting to listen and test the air.

The chill breeze was flowing upvalley. Wolf automatically sorted the mélange of animal odors. Potential prey registered first. Elk and deer were numerous—and a few moose. Traces of bighorn sheep. Worrisome was the absence of fresh wolf scent.

Time and again he digressed to inspect likely marking sites. Some had been used by a number of different wolves—but none recently. Nearing the valley floor, he strode out to traverse it at right angles. A spike-antlered bull elk bolted and careered into the trees, cracking and crashing through undergrowth and deadfall.

Several wolf trails threaded along the bottomland, but all scats and scents were old. Wolf easily cleared the small stream in the center of the valley and continued his reconnaissance. The far side yielded the same result. The pack that had formerly been resident was no longer active here. A group of moderate size, perhaps six to eight, Wolf guessed. Where had they gone—and why? Moving gradually upstream toward the junction of the three headwater basins, Wolf crossed and recrossed the main valley. Once he thought that he had detected a vestige of fresher scent, but he wasn't sure. Enthusiasm was fading into depression and discouragement.

Again at the creek bank, he stared into a gentle eddy flecked by spots of white foam. These traverses were fruitless. More would likely tell him nothing new. Perhaps the pack was temporarily restricting itself to the upper basins, although the area seemed much too small. He would explore their perimeters anyway. His dispirited jump fell slightly short, leaving a hind leg dangling in the water.

As he lunged up out of the channel and shook, a tiny chipmunk squeaked off through the grass. Wolf's legs trembled, wanting to bounce, pounce, and pin. But he followed the little rodent's speedy departure only with his eyes. Off to the shelter of a twisted stump. Beyond lay an expanse of dry grass bordered by Engelmann spruce. A shadow flickered behind their trunks. Movement!

Wolf raced upstream to the cover of trees, then circled sharply to intersect the animal's trail downwind. Had it been moving to the rear in order to investigate his own trail? He thought so. He flew through undergrowth and over logs in the dimming light. He hadn't run so fast since . . . Bitch! Twenty yards beyond the scent he finally braked to a jolting halt and wheeled in pursuit.

Passing the place where he had first noticed motion, Wolf slowed to a controlled gallop, then a trot. It wouldn't do to come charging up from behind unannounced. Or had he scared her off already? Now moving back downvalley he faced the wind. It was getting dark.

Just below the very slope he had descended into the cloverleaf basin, Wolf lost the scent. She had turned. His senses reached in all directions. Slowly he rotated his head. To the right. To the left. Watching him with interest from an aspen cluster sat a gray black wolf. A young bitch. Thin. With a badly torn ear. And a light gray stripe down the middle of her face.

THIRTEEN

He met her pale brown eyes for just a moment. The freshening breeze ruffled the two wolves' fur. A large, light snowflake blew across their line of sight. Then another.

Wolf turned his head back quickly, almost in a jerk, and faced straight ahead. But that made him more ill at ease. Why had he broken contact so abruptly? He wished to express calm and confidence, disguise his discomfort. Instead he developed a spasm of nervous shudders. Looking to infinity, he sniffed silently to find her scent. But she had placed herself downwind. Well, here I am. There she is. What do I do next? His tail drooped.

Wolf's apparent shyness and hesitation piqued the young bitch's curiosity. She had found the switchback trail he had left on the hillside upon entering the cloverleaf basin, and he certainly seemed to have been eager to overtake her. His manner conveyed nothing threatening or hostile, so she was not at all alarmed. He was indeed a large, handsome gray wolf. She decided to make the first move. Light snow was melting on the still warm ground. Rising slowly, she advanced a few steps and gently wagged her tail.

This simple positive gesture was all that was needed to dispel the immobilizing web of doubts and worries that had beset Wolf. In peripheral vision he recognized it immediately and at first reacted in a reflexive way. Still watching her from the corner of his eye, he reversed himself and began circling cautiously with the intention of approaching her upwind. The guard hairs of his shoulders and spine were elevated ever so slightly. But as soon as he was moving he relaxed and turned directly toward her in an easy lope.

Inhibitions melted progressively as he drew closer. His happy tail undertook such exaggerated waggings as to sway his entire hindquarters from side to side, giving his gait a conspicuously ungainly sort of waggle. He radiated contagiously honest delight.

She could not help responding favorably to this unusually warm greeting, even though the sudden change of tactics was puzzling. She too swung her tail briskly to and fro but stiffened somewhat when he confronted her. A snowflake entered her injured ear, causing it to flap embarrassingly. Touching moist noses softly, the pair nuzzled and sniffed to affirm their amiability. Although of questionable necessity, Wolf then proceeded with the traditional canine confirmation of gender, which the bitch passively—if not proudly—permitted. Shewolf! His long-range assessment had been correct.

Mindful that he was an intruder in territory where the young female had probably spent most of her life, and that the circumstances of their meeting had been out of the ordinary—if not obviously forced—Wolf was anxious to put her completely at ease and gain her confidence, especially because of the importance which he attached to their future relationship. Unsure of the best way of expressing himself, he suddenly flopped down in front of her like an impetuous puppy. Just as quickly he leapt up and dashed around her in a tight circle.

To his great relief, she seemed to share his exuberance and soon gave chase. He sprinted away from her in a wide arc across the meadow, then tried to stop and spin for a mischievous ambush of his pursuer. But he skidded out of control on the accumulating slush and fell flat on his side. Shewolf was no more successful in braking and tripped as she attempted to hurdle his sprawling form.

Both lay in the wet grass, panting and looking at each other. It was fun. Under clouds, the night was becoming very dark. The two wolves were openly happy to be together. They were innately affectionate; it had been unnatural for them to be alone. Snow continued to flurry unnoticed.

What happened to your ear?

I had a misunderstanding with another wolf. I tried to avoid her, but she had lost her temper and wanted to teach me a lesson.

One of the pack that was here?

Yes. The leader's mate.

Where have they gone?

Down to the foothills for the cold season—until the next puppies are old enough to travel. That's what caused our disagreement. I wanted to follow them down, but they wouldn't let me.

You weren't accepted?

No. But I stayed around them here. I was whelped in this valley. Why did you come? Why are you alone?

Wolf stood up and shook the moisture from his fur. He glanced about as if he had some important purpose in mind, but the pretense was quite unconvincing. He obviously couldn't see much. I've been alone for similar reasons. Differences with my home pack. But I don't intend to remain alone. I want to form a family group. That's why I came here. I came because I want you to join me.

The bitch sat up, genuinely surprised. What is so special about me? How did you know I existed? How did you find me?

The light snow was beginning to stick in the grass. Wolf waited a long time before replying. He walked slowly back and forth, occasionally glancing at his companion. He longed to confide in her, but he knew that he could not risk that now. Nevertheless, evasiveness and deception did not come easily to him.

A friend, an older dog who had spent considerable time in this valley, informed me of your situation. I guess that I'm impatient. I chose to seek you out rather than search aimlessly elsewhere. I hope that you will return with me across the mountains where my friend waits alone. We can each help the other through the time of snows. By the next warm season we can have our own famliy. Will you come?

He had stopped his pacing, and they were staring at one another. She did not respond. But Wolf thought that he understood her. Perhaps it was faith.

Let's go. And he started for the valley wall. She followed.

FOURTEEN

Wolf led her directly up to the shoulders of the massive mountain—the way he had come. Their progress over the rugged terrain was slow in the heavy darkness and wet snow. More than half the night had passed when they reached the northern rim of the deep river valley. Both were very tired. Wolf had not rested in three days; the young bitch was neither strong nor used to prolonged travel. After a painstaking, difficult descent into the canyon, they curled up back-to-back beneath a two-hundred-foot Douglas fir.

* * *

At once Wolf became aware of bright light penetrating his eyelids. Taking a first peek, he saw that the sky had cleared and the new snow was melting rapidly under midmorning sun. But something bothered him. What . . . ? He was alone!

In an instant he was sniffing Shewolf's resting place. She hadn't been gone long. Galloping along her trail toward the river, he nearly collided with her as she rounded a willow clump. Returning from the water, she was distinctly less fragrant than Wolf had remembered. Rotten trout!

Are you hungry?

Not wishing to imply any lack of ability to feed herself, Shewolf finally allowed that she had been thirsty and thought that an available snack would help to sustain her on their journey. Wolf was sensitive to her pride and tried not to communicate his reservations regarding the quality of her choice. Her bony frame made it clear that she was underfed. He would keep alert to opportunities for food along the way.

I could use a good meal—and some water. With that he trotted down to the bank and lapped up the cool liquid.

By early afternoon they had surmounted the steep south side of the canyon and stood atop the long ridge at the bend in the main range. Two days toward the morning sun lies a pass leading to the valley in which I left my friend. I hope that we'll find him there. He'll be glad to see us. Wolf was worried about Elder. He knew that the old dog could not survive another winter alone. Now that he and Shewolf were rested and well on their way, he did not want to waste time unnecessarily.

Except for an occasional drink, they pushed on without pause until evening of the next day. Wolf knew the route and so kept in the lead and set the pace. Most of the time Shewolf trotted right behind him—and did not complain. But late in the second afternoon she began to lag noticeably. Shortly after dark, Wolf turned into an aspen grove just a few hundred yards from the stream and sat down. She soon wandered in next to him and stood panting heavily, her breath fogging vertically into the still night air. When he leaned backward and stretched out on his side, she circled, lay down, and fell asleep in less than a minute.

* * *

There was just a hint of first light when Wolf rose silently and slipped away from his slumbering companion. Standing at the edge of a frosted meadow, he indulged in a deep yawn and a long, vibrating stretch. He felt the lazy alertness of earliest morning and, surveying the dimming eastern starfield, waited for his circulation to limber him. Wolf had a plan. First, his disguise.

As though activated by some unheard impulse, he wheeled to his left and loped over to a game path at the edge of the trees. He moved rapidly upvalley in a deceptively easy trot, constantly scrutinizing the air and glancing from side to side. He stopped short and raised his nose to sniff. The gentle airflow was wafting down the valley walls toward the stream. Bending his knees and elbows, he lowered his torso and stalked stealthily into the shadowy forest.

The sky was much lighter when he approached the limits of the lodgepole stand. Before him shimmered a circular pond half-covered by lily pads. The little basin, some fifty yards in diameter, was the mold of an ice chunk left by an ancient glacier. Humid air was steeped in moose scent. A small bat fluttered past his head—returning to its daylight seclusion. Even though he detected no large animal at the moment, Wolf was pleased. For there in the grass lay his steaming quarry. Fresh moose dung!

For a few seconds he stood relaxed, eyes closed, and enjoyed the powerful pungency of its full, rich odor. Then, remembering his early-morning mission, he strode deliberately to the droppings and rolled over in their midst. On his back, he squirmed and wriggled and kicked the air contentedly. At last satisfied by the extent of his newly acquired aroma, Wolf flipped himself upright, shook sparingly, and darted once again into the trees.

All stars had faded into the lightening grayness when he topped a bedrock hill not far from the aspens where Shewolf slept. He commanded a largely unobstructed view of nearly a mile of stream. His eyes followed it carefully. Close to the center of a long straight reach of water floated two large white spots. Back down the hill.

The trumpeter swans were unnerved not a little when Wolf came thrashing nonchalantly through the thicket of willows and plunged his forelegs noisily into the stream to drink. They felt some security in the fact that he was thirty yards upstream, but, being upwind of him, they had not suspected his presence and were startled to learn of it so suddenly. They elected to swim around a sweeping meander to a safer distance downstream.

Furtive glances kept Wolf apprised of their movements as he continued lapping loudly. The instant they glided out of sight, he streaked downvalley through the woods and cut over to intersect the stream just below the bend. Stalking catlike through grass to the water's edge, he crouched in the concealment of willows overhanging the deepest part of the channel.

Both swans ignored the strong scent of moose manure as they rounded the curve. One wisely paddled down the center of the waterway. The other, following the current, allowed itself to drift into deeper water within a few feet of the willow-fringed bank.

Wolf's quivering muscles were bunched up ready to spring. His target seemed to have slowed just to tease him. At last the unwary fowl floated into view: five feet to his left, two feet below him. He propelled himself straight out—just in front of and slightly above the bird.

At first motion the swan attempted to take off. To its astonishment, this resulted in a mid-air collision with a one-hundred-twenty-pound wolf. The two animals plunged into the fountaining stream beneath an explosion cloud of white feathers. While still underwater, Wolf managed to secure his prey by the neck, and the outcome of the incident was decided. Wolf never saw the other swan again.

* * *

The smooth hues of a cloudless sunrise had progressed into pale grayish blue when Shewolf arose and shook clinging aspen leaves from her fur. Casually sniffing and casting about for Wolf, she was not concerned about his absence. He must have gone for a drink. The scent of a doe and fawn excited her. She was ready to begin hunting when the air brought another blend of smells. The association of moose dung, swan, and dog wolf was new to her nose. So she moved to the edge of the grove for a better sample.

Prancing proudly into the dawn sunlight emerged the successful hunter: head high, chest heaving, the wet swan slung across his dripping shoulders. In his haste to deliver the bounty, Wolf had neglected to shake himself properly. Dropping the deceased bird to the ground, he stood before Shewolf feeling quite satisfied. His drenched coat displayed an unusual mosaic of matted moose manure overlaid by white feathers. She considered him skeptically for a moment. It seemed that the distinction between aroma and stench had a great deal to do with state of mind. Then she went about the business of feeding herself.

FIFTEEN

By noon the two wolves were approaching the tundra slopes leading up to the divide. Wolf surveyed the high basin in search of bighorn rams but saw none. Just below the pass they encountered a series of deep snowbanks. Much had melted but, because the remainder was thinly crusted and difficult to negotiate, the pair followed a weaving course between the drifts. As they moved toward the crest, Wolf watched the monolith beneath which he had flushed a ptarmigan. It looked entirely different now. Would Shewolf ever believe his story? Would she even tolerate it?

The descent of the high eastern slope was long and tiring for the bitch: steep, lumpy tundra and vast boulder fields. But compared to his previous crossing, it was easy for Wolf. They finally reached the long timbered ridge on the north side of the valley and paused to rest. Wolf introduced her to the beaver ponds and elk meadows which they could now see below them. And the slope on the far side where he had left his friend. Anxious to find the old dog before dark, Wolf rose and moved on. It was dusk when they jumped the stream a mile above the dams.

Are there other wolves in this valley?

None that I've detected. Just Elder.

Then that must be he.

Her nose held high, Shewolf turned to her left, downwind. Less than a hundred yards downstream sat Elder. He was erect and motionless atop a low bluff on their side of the channel. Next to the contorted skeleton of a lodgepole pine, the old gray wolf might have been a weather-worn stump in the fading light.

The moment Wolf fixed him, Elder jumped forward and trotted eagerly around the rim to welcome the pair. Wolf bounded toward him. Their tails started wagging simultaneously, and, upon meeting, they sniffed each other thoroughly as if each was unsure of the other's identity.

I see that you were successful.

Yes. Shewolf has come to join us. Elder moved calmly to her side, letting her know that he was pleased to be with her. She was cautiously friendly at first, but the old one's poised, natural manner quickly put her at ease. And she recognized the dog scent that she had several times encountered in her home valley.

You're back sooner than I expected. I was worried about the storm when you crossed the pass.

I was lucky to make it. I had some remarkable experiences. Elder cocked his head. I was completely blinded by snow and clouds going over the top. Then I met Rufus.

Rufus!? How is that possible? Did you lose consciousness?

No. Just the opposite. It's important for you to know what I've learned. Busy sniffing out a badger hole, Shewolf looked up curiously but then returned to her investigations.

Elder glanced at the young bitch. I gather that she is not totally aware of your intentions.

No, not yet. One thing at a time. But how have you been? Was the storm severe? Have you food?

I am well. The snow was light down here. As you can see, most of it has melted. The storm appeared to have been concentrated up along the peaks. The elk has kept—there is still enough for you both. He looked again at the female. You two must be famished. Let's go eat.

At this Shewolf backed out of the musky burrow, straightening up expectantly. Having swallowed more feathers than meat at her last meal, the prospect of

wapiti for dinner made her drool in anticipation. The three wolves started downvalley.

Stars were filling the darkening sky as the trio trotted in close rank diagonally across the field toward the far fringe of forest. Excited by the promise of new territory and new relationships, Shewolf hurried ahead to explore the periphery of the grassy expanse. Slowing to a steady walk, Wolf related the details of his journey and visions to his politely receptive ally.

When they reached the elk, Elder sat down, panting lightly, and contentedly watched the other two consume what was left of the remaining hindquarter. Full and weary—and suddenly very sleepy—Shewolf moved away and curled up on a bed of pine needles.

Wolf felt thoroughly good. Even his physical fatigue was satisfying; he was full of confidence. The night breeze hushing through the treetops seemed to settle turmoils of the past and whisper the promise of the future. Once again Wolf knew a longing to express himself, his happiness: a burgeoning urge to sing. This time he gave in to his emotions. Despite a signal of caution from Elder, he raised his muzzle to the sky, slowly closing his eyes, and sent an impassioned, trailing call thrilling across the valley. It had been so long.

Sensing his mistake too late, he looked back to Shewolf. She was gone. He saw her trotting off into the darkness, which seemed to be deepening.

SIXTEEN

As he became fully aware of what had happened, Wolf felt like biting himself—or running into a tree. He was utterly disgusted, beset by shock waves of fright and despair. He could only sit and stare as She-wolf moved into the night. Even before she was lost to view, Wolf no longer saw her. His eyes had opened to infinity; his mind had clouded in a turbulent jumble of thoughts. The night seemed black in the absolute.

How could he have been so stupid, so unthinking? Everything had been going so well. He had become overconfident, too sure of the inevitable success of his plans. He had lost his perspective, given in to himself, relaxed the control he had imposed so carefully for so long. What could he do now? Could he possibly undo the effects of his inexcusable blunder? Would Shewolf stop? Would she reconsider? Or would she return to her cloverleaf valley? He trembled. Where would he find another mate? How long would it take? He could not tolerate the thought of missing the next season of puppies. A distant sound caught his attention. Not so distant. No—right next to him. Elder snorted again. He was standing at Wolf's side.

The old dog was annoyed by Wolf's actions. Not because of his own conditioned distaste for song—he was beginning to appreciate that singing was something true and beautiful for Wolf—but because of Wolf's lapse of judgment. And now his indecisiveness, paralysis. He had tried to warn Wolf at the last minute but had been ignored. In spite of these feelings, Elder did not want to chastise his friend, to communicate disapproval. This was a time for encouragement.

You had better decide what to do right away.

Wolf turned, panting, ears back. But he avoided Elder's forceful gaze. How could I have been so foolish?

Stop worrying about what has already happened. And stop feeling sorry for yourself. The damage is not irreparable. What is the best thing to do *now*?

Elder sat down: waiting, holding his eyes intently upon Wolf.

The other ceased panting in a series of slurps and looked up to the sky, ears again erect. Once more he realized the indefinable beauty of the firmament. He faced Elder. I doubt that she will travel far. She is heavy with food and very tired. We can find her. I am certain of that. Wolf's whiskers twitched nervously.

Elder sighed. The problem is, of course, to do so without alarming her or alienating her further. Understand her reactions. You disillusioned her. She joined you and came here because of natural desire to share her life. You appeal to her. She would be your mate, mother to your puppies. You had given her no reason to expect anything unusual from you—let alone behavior she was undoubtedly taught to regard as immoral and demeaning. Now she must feel deceived and betrayed. And surely she mistrusts you. At best she is bewildered and confused. Don't compound your mistake by overlooking these things.

Wolf rose and began pacing in a small semicircle, staring blankly at the ground. He knew that he needed Elder's help. And he was confident of his friend's willingness to do all that he could. Even so, he hesitated. He was not ashamed to ask. It was just that . . . it would have been so much more satisfying, he would have been so proud, if he could have handled the situation smoothly by himself. A vole popped up in curiosity from its hole in front of him. And just as quickly snapped back down like a tiny, bewhiskered jack-in-the-box. Wolf paused and watched for a moment, then turned to Elder.

Will you go after her? Will you explain to Shewolf that, that . . .

That you are a normal wolf? A suitable mate?

Yes.

I shall try, but I am uncertain about how and even whether that can be accomplished. We've just met. She knows you far better than she knows me. How can I gain her confidence? She may simply dismiss me as your subordinate doing your bidding.

Wolf squinted slightly, penetrating Elder's concerned expression. He sensed a reversal of initiative. His momentary helplessness had passed. Renewed confidence and resolve fed upon themselves and he moved a little closer. Elder, Shewolf was comfortable with you —she liked you. And it wasn't you who sang. She will believe you.

Perhaps. The old wolf peered into the valley. That will depend upon how much I ask her to believe. It's difficult to know how much she can accept. There will be a critical threshold. How would you have me approach the subject?

Eyes glistening in the starlight, Wolf seated himself before his companion. He shifted and shivered with restless energy. The excitement of sudden certainty, of being sure. Of realizing a personal reality. As if a clear, profound message had been released in his mind. A message of his song.

Let Shewolf know the simple truth. The truth as you perceive it, Elder—from your point of view. Recount the story of our meeting, of your reactions to song, of your dreams and changing attitudes, of your continuing doubts. She is young. Surely she will open her mind enough to judge for herself.

And what of the truth as *you* perceive it? Your visits with Dirus? Your visions of the past, of Rufus and all the rest?

Wolf inhaled the night air. The breeze had lulled. Crisp quiet in the mountain valley seemed to invite—indeed, implore—song. No, she can learn of those experiences only from me. They have been mine. That will take time—and care. I have certainly learned that tonight. Relearned it. I shall not err in that way again.

And what of your determination to sire puppies, to teach them to sing? Through them to promote song among all wolves?

That must be between Shewolf and myself. I can only hope to bring her to a position of receptive neutrality. I believe . . . I know that the puppies will teach her. Given a chance, they will teach all of us.

A faint whiff of black bear. Wolf eased up and circled silently, but the still air gave no hint of direction. A young boar, he judged. Probably a two-year-old in his first season alone. Elder rose and bowed to stretch his forelegs. His lengthy yawn ended audibly in what sounded very much like a brief, muted song. Wolf smiled inwardly. The noises of a heavy animal running up the slope above them signaled that the bear had been closer than they suspected. He had evidently scented the elk carcass.

The two wolves sniffed each other for a moment, tails flagging their affection. Elder's optimism was guarded; Wolf's was full of faith. And Elder trotted off along Shewolf's trail, his wise old nose close to the ground.

SEVENTEEN

The moonless night was cold and calm. But not so Wolf. He had curled up to sleep in half a dozen different spots but nevertheless remained keenly alert. After his almost week-long journey through the mountains, he was far from caught up in his rest. Ordinarily he would have slept easily. Why must this night be so deathly still? So empty and devoid of distractions? So conducive to thought?

At length he again pulled himself to his feet and ambled over to the vole's burrow. The little rodent had mustered enough courage to make several forays while Wolf had been lying down—and watching. At the moment he was in residence. Wolf raked half-heartedly around the entrance. Then a thorough sniffing. No change. Dirt in his nostrils caused Wolf to sneeze with authority. This encouraged the vole to spurt three feet deeper into the tunnel.

For two hours Wolf sat in a small clearing on the hillside. The starfield revolved imperceptibly about the northern sky above a great dark mass of rock. Even in silhouette its top resembled the upper part of an owl. At intervals, Wolf's head jerked and cocked to various angles as he traced white-hot trails of meteors burning through the sky. How can the night be so long? Elder might have been back by now if Shewolf had not gone far—and if she had been approachable, and agreeable. But then, if she were still traveling the old dog might not yet have overtaken her.

Wolf sighed. His limbs were relaxed and feeling the gentle ache of fatigue. He looked at the place where Shewolf had rested so recently. He thought of trying to sleep there. It might bring good fortune. No, upon returning she might prefer her former bed—or she might associate it with hearing his song and avoid it. Worried and tired, Wolf no longer knew which superstitions and suspicions to follow. He needed rest.

Finally stretching out where he was, he closed his eyes and forced himself to think happy thoughts. Of racing through green meadow, tall limber grass brushing and slapping his face. Dashing after startled ground squirrels. Of a gigantic, distorted full moon bulging blood red over a dusky horizon. Of wrestling a littermate to its back and feeling another shake his hind leg with would-be savage snarls. Of cooling rain on a hot sagebrush afternoon. Of puppies singing freely. He was asleep.

* * *

Elder fought with the confidence of his prime. Spinning and lunging in defense, he repeatedly thwarted thrusts by the five wolves that surrounded him. But his spirit only magnified the imminent tragedy. He had little chance. Diversionary jabs would draw his attention as he was hit simultaneously from the opposite sides. In a final desperate charge to break out of the circle, he . . .

* * *

Wolf's heart was pounding. His eyes blinked open. He waited for his senses to sharpen. The sun was about to rise. He had slept for several hours. Was the excitement he felt due solely to the dream, or had something really happened? He concentrated with an intensity bordering on discomfort—trying to resolve the situation without moving, without looking. The dawn air carried the answer: Elder and Shewolf had returned!

Uncertainty froze him. What was his wisest

course of action? Motionless, he drew from the atmosphere all the information it could yield him. The old dog was awake, resting close behind Wolf. He had been back for quite a while. Shewolf was asleep under trees some distance away. Relief and delight buoyed him. He harnessed an urge to rush to the others, to her. To explain his actions and feelings, to display his affection. He knew now that Elder and Shewolf gave something more essential, more personal and basic to his life than simple companionship.

What had happened? How had she responded to Elder's entreaties? He must know these things before approaching Shewolf. He must consult with Elder. And even as these thoughts flowed, the old dog rose silently and padded to Wolf's side. You were right. I think she did believe me. She wants to trust you. Let's go down for a drink.

At the sharp report of a beaver's tail, several dozen Canadian geese abruptly ended their overnight stay in a dramatic mass takeoff. From the edge of the pond Wolf and Elder viewed the spectacle of splashing and flapping as the flock became airborne in the westerly breeze and then, climbing, circled back down-valley toward the plains and a large, orange sun.

Wolf had his own drinking rhythm. Lap . . . lap . . . lap, lap, lap. Lap . . . lap . . . lap, lap, lap. Elder's was less regular. Slurp, slurp . . . slurp. Slurp, slurp, slurp . . . slurp. She wasn't as disillusioned by you as

I expected—or perhaps as she should have been. It was mainly the shock of the event rather than any inferences she might've drawn about you. It was something entirely new, something she had never considered. She simply didn't understand.

Wolf raised his dripping muzzle and regarded Elder in amazement. Do you mean that her reaction was not totally negative? Not like yours and the others'?

That's right. I was surprised too. His thirst satisfied, Elder backed away from the bank and belched. He spied a trout leaping for a morning moth near the middle of the pond. Shewolf has had a very unusual life. She was fortunate to have survived. Elder walked leisurely to a grassy bluff and sat down, licking his lips.

Wolf watched for a moment, then trotted after him. The ascending sun was now yellow white and growing smaller. What was so unusual? You mean being alone?

It's *why* she has been alone. When she was still a small puppy, for some reason her mother decided to move the litter to an alternate den a long distance away. She took Shewolf first and then went back for the others—but she never returned.

And Shewolf couldn't find her way back?

No. She had barely been weaned. To this day she has not learned what happened to her family.

Wolf lay down on his stomach, extending his legs

forward and back. Holding Elder's gaze, he rested his head on forepaws. How did she live? Was she adopted by others?

Just by luck as far as I was able to determine. She wandered around and foraged for herself. Somehow she was able to avoid predators and scavenge enough to subsist. Before her first cold season she crossed the path of a larger group in the cloverleaf drainage and followed them down to the foothills. She's been trailing them ever since. Living largely on their leavings. As you know, they did not accept her.

Wolf blinked. He blinked again. What about song?

It seems that she was almost completely deprived of schooling in the ways of wolves. Everything from vital necessities like hunting techniques to the rules of social status and taboos of personal behavior. Elder shook his head, sprinkling a few droplets of water into Wolf's face.

Wolf stood. His tail swayed slowly. Shewolf doesn't know that song is wrong?

Oh, she knows. She knows that it is condemned. But she doesn't feel it. It's foreign to her. She's heard coyotes. But she has had no personal experience with other wolves' reactions. Elder fairly glared at his younger companion. By some incredible chance, Shewolf is morally uninstructed, ignorant.

Unconditioned! Wolf asserted himself. Open-minded. Free! That is not ignorant; that is natural. I trust that you did not feel compelled . . .

Ka-chunk! The sound of weight plunged into water. Wolf and Elder turned together. Fifty feet to their left was Shewolf, standing shoulder-high in the pond and looking down disappointedly at the wake of an elusive fish. Wolf lurched backward and butted Elder playfully into the grass. Then he gaited clumsily but happily toward the young bitch.

Having arranged herself comfortably next to a spray of willows, she did her best to seem startled as Wolf approached. That slowed and stopped him. He avoided her eyes at first.

EIGHTEEN

Winter along the edge of the eastern foothills was difficult. But, hunting together, the three wolves found enough food and were able to enjoy the beauties of the snow season. Elder was stronger than when he and Wolf had first met. Although he could not regain quickness and agility, his long and varied experience led him to suggest many successful strategies which he himself could no longer implement. Shewolf actually gained weight during this time when most wolves lose. And she learned rapidly, soon becoming a competent hunter. She was a fast runner for short distances and worked well in concert with Wolf.

For a long period after Elder had persuaded Shewolf to return, Wolf did not sing. He was reluctant to broach the subject at all. But by the time the trio migrated to the foothills, he had become sufficiently confident of the strength of his bond with Shewolf and of her relative indifference to singing that he was able to convince himself to be more honest. It was not an easy step. He did not want to jeopardize their relationship in any way. But the season of mating was approaching; this exerted constant pressure on him because he wanted Shewolf to be reconciled to his beliefs before that time. Elder's passive tolerance helped.

As the span of daylight once again began to lengthen and the sun's path moved gradually northward, Wolf adopted a pattern of occasional singing in private—at some distance from his companions. Nonetheless, they could hear him and knew that it was he. Initially he was very apprehensive, worrying about adverse reaction. But there was none. And soon he found that a lack of response can be as frustrating as hostility. He became bolder, singing whenever his spirit moved him and expressing his feelings more and more freely. His concern diminished with time. He felt as though his soul had again been released, that he could once more be true to himself. It had a positive effect on all of his behavior. Shewolf and Elder could not help noticing this.

Wolf developed a fairly regular habit of singing during the hours of dusk and before starting on hunting excursions. Sending his voice into the sky never failed to exhilarate and inspire him. It was a special means, a very positive and satisfying means of affirming reverence for his world. A farewell to the retired sun, an eager acceptance of the challenge of existence. At such times he often recalled his very first song. He had been so nervous, so excited. And he thought of all that Dirus had taught.

Inasmuch as he sang freely now, he was often in view of Elder and Shewolf and was not averse to taking furtive, squinting glances at his companions while actually singing. Elder studiously avoided watching Wolf. Invariably the old dog tried to give the impression of focusing his attention on something else—usually something distant. He would wear a blank or mildly pained expression. It was as though his tolerance of song—indeed, his growing understanding and appreciation of it—represented a concession, a change of such import and magnitude that it required for the sake of pride a suppression of all superficial manifestation. Shewolf, however, did look at Wolf as he sang. Sometimes in apparent puppy-like bewilderment and curiosity. Again, with an aspect of intense concern.

A layer of extremely frigid air flowed over the plains and into mountain valleys. A breath of the arctic. It was colder than Wolf could remember. Elder recalled days as cold or colder in his youth. Early-morning snow had decorated the landscape. It squeaked under Wolf's feet. This delighted him so much that he walked back and forth in front of their sleeping places at least thirty times. Just to hear it. Elder looked on, his eyelids drooping in drowsiness.

By midday the sky had cleared to a diffuse, frosty blue. And although it was free of definite clouds, there continued a gentle rain of little hexagonal flakes. Intricately symmetrical, infinitely varied, perfectly preserved. Crystallizing air. A thin, high film of ice cloud conjured a brilliant Sun Dog: a broad, bright halo about the sun with two diametrically opposed peripheral orbs. Wolf noticed it by chance. Three suns! For many minutes he stood in awe and stared. His eyes followed the ring, avoiding the sun itself. He had never seen anything of its kind. To him it seemed both to proclaim the magnificence of its own being and to presage a glorious future. He accepted it as a powerful omen.

Soon thereafter Wolf began spending more and more time with Shewolf, following her around, keeping track of her whereabouts even when they were not actually together. At the same time he became slightly resentful of Elder and occasionally irritable with him. But the old wolf understood and did not mind. Although he could no longer be in competition with Wolf as a suitor, the younger dog's reaction was natural. Shewolf was now sexually mature and coming into her first season.

* * *

Winter dawn was almost always cold, but fresh and pleasing. Wolf lay tightly curled, a ball of warm gray in the snow. His luxuriant tail fluffed over his paws and nose. Lazy comfort; a delightful, sensual coziness. He enjoyed it, at intervals snuggling into even more satisfying positions. It seemed that he might so indulge himself indefinitely. But, watching Shewolf's breath stream upward, he soon became restless. And he was no longer content.

He raised his head to look directly at her, and, without conscious decision, began a prolonged series of soft, mellow whimpers. A gentle, undulating sort of wowing, conveying both pleading desire and strong conviction. His eyes glistened with intensity, imploring response. Her ears alerted and turned; her eyes opened and rolled toward him. But that was all.

Early white-gold sunlight streaked through chilling overcast. Elder continued to sleep and snore. At length Wolf eased to his feet and moved quietly to Shewolf's side. Lowering his head, he tenderly nuzzled her neck, behind her ear. She closed her eyes and, tilting her head slightly away to encourage his attention, uttered a barely audible squeak of pleasure. He delicately nibbled the side of her mouth, then licked her muzzle and entire face. She returned his affection in kind. The scent that now enveloped her told Wolf that the season of mating had begun.

Overcome by excitement, he bolted away and raced frantically around in erratic circles. Pulling up short, he turned his head in a jerk and eyed Shewolf with a wildly capricious expression. His tail was wagging strenuously. Without warning he bounded to her and flopped down on forelegs in playful challenge. Sweeping his muzzle to one side, he gave a mischievous woof. Elder lifted his head with exaggerated effort as though annoyed at being awakened. And promptly sneezed.

At this Wolf plunged his nose beneath Shewolf's chest in an attempt to nudge her to her feet. But, suddenly aloof, she declined to rise. Abandoning this tactic, he took the more direct approach of trying to uplift her from the rear. At once she leapt forward, wheeled, and, tucking her tail between her legs, seated herself with an air of adamant indifference.

Wolf stared at her for a few moments. His ears and tail drooped. He knew it simply might not be her natural time of receptivity, but this understanding did little to assuage his disappointment or diminish his eagerness and impatience. Nor could he entirely suppress the fear that Shewolf did have reservations regarding his suitability as sire of her whelps, reservations that could inhibit normal reactions. And why did Elder have to be watching? As if the old dog were somehow at fault, Wolf gave him a quick glance of irritation before ambling dejectedly back to his resting place.

In the days that followed Wolf and Shewolf stayed close together more than ever before. Preoccupied by their increasingly intimate relationship, Wolf had lost all interest in food and hunting. Numerous times each day the two freely displayed their feelings for one another. But, despite repeated amorous advances by Wolf, Shewolf remained unwilling to culminate their courtship.

Reluctantly, Wolf began to consider the possibility that she would never receive him. And he continued to worry about all sorts of reasons for their incompatibility. He had initially thought that she might hesitate to rear puppies in the presence of a singing sire. So he had promised Shewolf not to influence them to song by example—corrupt them by singing was an alternative characterization according to Elder. Wolf was sure that song was inborn and would surface in the pups naturally. He would wait for their initiative. In return, Shewolf agreed not to do anything to discourage their singing should it develop. Elder took no part in this. It was all he could do to conceal his curiosity and anxiety.

Having learned from Elder of Wolf's violent experiences when first he sang, Shewolf had expressed concern about the potential danger of other wolves attacking their family in outrage over song. In honesty, Wolf could not assure her of absolute safety in this regard, but he did emphasize that it was highly unlikely so long as they maintained their own warm-season territories when the whelps were young, and roamed their cold-season range always together and with care not to infringe upon the activities of other groups. The right of territory and respect for group and family unity were far more important to wolves, he believed, than any prejudice resulting from instruction. Moreover, once the first litter had matured, their numbers would be sufficient for protection in any event. He had not yet confided to her his knowledge of what had happened in the days of Rufus.

* * *

It was an unseasonably mild afternoon. Warming chinook winds from the mountains temporarily brought the balmy temperatures of spring. Remnants of snow were quickly consumed. Wolf noticed a subtle change in Shewolf's gait as she rounded a clump of dry brush and trotted toward him. Elder must have sensed something too for he was sitting rigidly alert and watching with unusual interest—even excitement. She began whimpering softly as she drew near, and Wolf's excitement grew far beyond that of Elder.

Rising on hind legs, Shewolf placed her forepaws across Wolf's shoulders and gently nipped his ear. Turning to face her, he also rose and they engaged each other in a flurry of clumsy sparring. To his surprise, she suddenly broke away and gave the long-awaited signal with a quick sideways sweep of her tail. The ardor of Wolf's response, however, surprised her not at all. He accepted this new challenge enthusiastically and with vigor. And soon they were coupled in the canine embrace of creation.

NINETEEN

For several days the two shared every waking hour. Even in sleep they lay stretched out side by side or nestled against each other in mutual warmth. Like puppies still apprehensive of the night seeking security in body contact. But they knew no apprehension. Theirs was now a soft, private world, one of new sensitivity and joy. Everything was special.

Among the high plains and foothills the season of new growth was beginning its annual struggle for succession. Invasions of severe cold had ended and

temperate interludes became longer. Another time of transition. As if unwilling to yield passively, however, the snows that did come fell more heavily and thickly, accumulating to greater depths.

Of necessity, the three wolves were on the move almost constantly in search of food, rarely pausing in one locality for more than a few days. This wandering life of winter took them across and around and throughout a very large area. The prey that they were able to catch did not provide enough to sustain them for long. An occasional straggling deer. And Shewolf's appetite was steadily increasing. Elder pretended to be indignant, chiding her for her gastronomical excesses. Especially for her growing habit of gnawing and consuming bone. Too much bone powder, he contended, would lead to inflexibility of the tail.

Late one afternoon the upslope breeze brought a blanket of billowing gray clouds. They rolled in against the ridges that bordered the mountains, hanging low and dark. The air was damp and chilly, full of the scent of snow. The storm broke like a wave, instantly obscuring all in whiteness. The three wolves curled up together beneath clustered pines on the lee of a hill. Unlike most spring snowfalls, this one streamed with the wind. At first wet and heavy, the large flakes plastered and coated every exposed surface. But as the temperature gradually decreased, the snow began to drift. Wolf wriggled himself closer to

Shewolf. He knew that the storm would be long, and he worried about hunting.

On the third day it ended. The sky lightened and parted into plumes of white in clear blue. Shrouds of smooth gray stubbornly clung to the tops of higher ridges along the mountain front. Eager to seek other creatures emerging from shelter, Wolf sprang from his mold, shook vigorously, and undertook a lengthy sequence of calisthenic stretches. Shewolf had just risen and was eating snow when he trotted off to explore the neighborhood. Elder looked on, peering thoughtfully from his small nose hole.

Wolf was relieved to find that most rises and windward slopes were only thinly covered so that traveling was easier than he had expected. In low places and on leeward slopes, however, the snow was banked in very deep, bulky drifts. Given a little luck, this situation might be turned to advantage. Much encouraged, the opportunistic hunter trotted diagonally into the wind toward the edge of an elongate mesa reaching out to the east.

Shewolf and Elder were watching a snowshoe hare scampering among trees on their right. It suddenly stopped, rose to a half-standing position on huge hind feet, then darted back under snow-draped brush. In a moment Wolf came into view loping toward his companions in a straight line. He was obviously bringing news. As they trotted to meet him, Shewolf gave a faint squeak. Wolf replied with a low, rolling call. He bounded right through the snowshoe tracks, ignoring the fresh scent. The three came together, moist noses touching, their tails radiating outward and wagging excitement.

Deer?

No, bison. An old bull on the next mesa. He's alone. Perhaps an outcast or some sort of renegade—or he may have become separated from his herd during the storm. If we can stalk him in just the right way, we'll all eat well and won't have to travel again for a long time.

Something seemed to bother Shewolf but she hesitated and did not communicate her concern. Elder was pessimistic. A bull bison is no easy quarry. Especially for just three wolves—including an old dog like myself and a mated bitch. With this Wolf spun around and galloped back the way he had come. Shewolf and Elder followed in customary single file.

The solitary buffalo was enormous. His legs seemed too short and thin for the massive bulk of his body. Working along a low rise near the north rim of the broad flat-topped ridge, he was attempting to scrape a thin cover of wind-blown snow from dry grass underneath. His right foreleg pawed and raked the ground, throwing up a cloud of white powder. Much of it settled on his back.

The wolves watched from the concealment of

trees a quarter of a mile to the south. A slight cross-wind drifted upslope toward the west. Elder's analysis was not encouraging. He's out in the open. It will be difficult to approach him undetected. But Wolf was confident. They would give his plan a try.

Shewolf and Elder started off. Retracing their paths, they plunged about halfway down the heavily drifted south slope of the plateau to the crest of a low shoulder. A narrow strip on its top had blown relatively free of snow. Turning left, they paced rapidly along this rise parallel to the rim of the bluff above. Thus shielded from the buffalo's view, the two moved eastward toward the forested front of the mesa. Once there, they would cross over to the north side. Wolf felt a little guilty about the route he had suggested, for in order to keep out of sight and minimize the chances of being scented they would have to struggle through very heavy snow.

He continued watching the old bull. It would take Shewolf and Elder a long time to move into position. The sky had cleared to pure blue, and the snow was softening under warming late-morning sun. Movement would cause no sound. The bison periodically interrupted his excavating to look around and test the air. As he exhaled, twin jets of white vapor issued from great dilated nostrils and rolled upward.

At one point the bull seemed to be disturbed by a scent. He turned into the wind, arching his ponderous head upward. But soon he returned to his chore of uncovering grass. The breeze had faded into a soft, indefinite flow—a calmness of little use in scenting. Wolf hoped that this good luck would swing the balance in favor of a successful approach by his comrades. He padded to a stumpy ponderosa, marked it, and moved down onto the south slope.

He turned to the right along the thinly covered shoulder. By now patches of moist brown earth were exposed. Nearing the west end of the mesa, Wolf angled back up to its top and passed silently through trees to the north rim. Here he doubled back to the east and cautiously began his stalk. The scattered stand of pines was thinning. He slowed to a deliberate foot-by-foot walk, bobbing his head from side to side as he moved in an effort to glimpse the buffalo in low corridors of light between the dark trunks. But he did not see him. So he stopped. There was still much time.

Wolf vibrated with the excitement of his first hunts as a gangling puppy. The physical demands of stalking and testing large prey were always great. To meet them there developed extraordinary stimulation, sure strength making possible exceptional effort. A special chemistry seeming to attune all senses far beyond their normal limits—charging them to a higher level of consciousness. Fully open, bristling sensitivity.

His head turned slowly. At once he was looking

at everything, focusing on nothing. It seemed as if he were absorbing simultaneously almost the entire sphere of sensory signals about him. Then he noticed the trees. The snow-laden ponderosas. His perception of them rose into inspiring acuity. He beheld creations of powerful beauty. Strong limbs extending in all directions, branching into cushioning sprays of long needles, all thickly overlaid by soft, rounding white. Smooth, billowing arms reaching one above the other, gradually shortening to give the whole a full cone-like form. Shafts of sun streaming through the whitened trees sparkled from countless crystals with mirror light. As he watched, moistening snow near the top of a tree to his right slipped from its cradling branches and plummeted downward causing an explosive chain reaction; a showering cascade of glistening powder. A fleeting shudder spread through Wolf's body, the same kind of tingling that he so often felt when singing. His forelegs trembled with nervous energy.

He wasn't sure if there had actually been a scent. But Wolf knew that a bobcat near the base of the ridge behind him had just ambushed a hare at the entrance of its burrow. And he knew that Shewolf and Elder were fighting their way through the upper part of a deep snowbank just below the north rim of the mesa several hundred yards beyond the bison. Wolf advanced. He could smell the bull now; the air was moving slightly. How soon would the scent of Shewolf and Elder reach the buffalo? Wolf paused at the edge of the trees above the north slope. A low mound of brown color barely loomed over the near horizon. It moved—back and forth. The bison's hump. His motions showed that he was still foraging. Not yet alarmed.

Shewolf stood just below the top of the bluff. She was waiting for Elder to catch up. In a moment he pushed in against her, shoulder deep in wet snow. Both were panting heavily. They relaxed there for many minutes. Once they topped the mesa there would be no time for rest. As their wind returned they mouthed a little snow for refreshment. Shewolf humped her back to stretch her legs and prepared to climb over the rim. She and Elder exchanged a final glance, then sprang onto the mesa.

They plunged a few yards straight away from the edge along which a lip of drifted snow curled over the top of the bluff. Once in shallower depths they swung to the right and began trotting westward parallel to the rim. They had gauged the bison's position well. He was about one hundred fifty yards ahead with his back to them and still pawing up snow. If they had tried to move closer out of sight, he might have scented them without their knowing it and started moving before they were able to give chase.

The distance had shortened by about half when the old bull raised his head to inhale and then snorted. The instant he began to turn, both wolves broke into full run. Elder galloped directly toward the bison, straining to reach the end of the low rise where the snow was thinner. He thrilled to be hunting once more, but how slow and awkward he felt. Shewolf angled slightly to the left in a headlong race to outflank the bull and prevent his moving toward the center of the mesa.

The old buffalo watched them for several moments, aiming his head first at one, then the other as though his eyes could look only straight ahead. His massiveness was imposing but his expression did not suggest significant insight. Mainly a sort of mindless bovine bewilderment. Finally reaching some kind of decision, he turned toward the rapidly approaching Shewolf and began pawing up quantities of snow and topsoil. Then he lowered his head and swung it from side to side in a rolling motion so that his curved horns hooked close to the ground.

Just as Shewolf was about to cut off his direct escape route to the interior of the mesa, the bull started trotting in that very direction. She pushed to her ultimate speed, flinging herself in great leaps over the snow. But as she was about to launch herself on one of these, a buried log bent her forelegs and somersaulted her forward onto her back under a shower of white. This inadvertent maneuver seemed to startle the bison, for he swerved and trotted heavily off to the right, directly away from Elder and parallel to the north rim.

Elder was tiring and had slowed to a moderate

lope along the rise pawed up by the buffalo. Still, he gradually shortened the distance and was soon close enough to risk an occasional nip at the bull's haunches and rump. This elicited some erratic backward kicking and a few threatening turns of the head.

Shewolf pulled herself up slowly, shook, and rejoined the pursuit. She gradually accelerated back to an open run and moved to reestablish her flanking position. The bison, however, allowed her to catch up almost immediately. Jerking to a halt, he dropped his head, braced himself on spindly front legs, and with unwieldly effort kicked both back legs out in a frantic buck. This took Elder by surprise and he had to brake so fast that he sat down. But he stopped in time to avoid the swinging hooves.

The abortive counterattack was apparently such a strain that the old bull decided to abandon the tactic and move on. Just as he started up, Shewolf turned in behind him and leapt up to secure a deep bitehold in his left buttock. A strenuous kick brushed her into the snow but not before she had inflicted sharp pain from the rear. The bison lunged forward into a jolting gallop. The two wolves renewed the chase, worrying him continually and doing all that they could to encourage his flight along the north side of the tableland. Shewolf pulled up next to him so that the bull could see her from the corner of his eye. This kept him from turning toward her, and the three galloped on just inside the rim toward a scattered stand of snow-clad ponderosa.

Hurling himself up from a flat crouch just twenty yards in front and slightly to the left of the onrushing bison, Wolf charged directly at him. It was a calculated risk, one to which he had not been willing to subject his mate or companion. The old bull just might accept the challenge. Shewolf turned in from the side, snapping at the buffalo's shoulder, while Elder made one last lunge at his rump. Wolf's sudden appearance was so unnerving that the bison reacted reflexively. Turning to the right, away from his three pursuers, he attempted a descent of the north slope. But when he jumped from the top of the bluff, he dropped heavily into an enormous, bulky drift. His thin legs were driven four feet into the great bank, and he was hopelessly mired.

The three wolves and the buffalo knew that the end of his declining years had been decided with the whoosh of his plunge into the snow. Shewolf had no difficulty in satisfying her deep hunger that evening as a new moon followed the sun over the horizon.

Shortly after dark Wolf reclimbed the mesa. He passed through the ponderosas and came to the western rim. There he sat and sang to the mountains.

TWENTY

For the first time that winter Wolf, Shewolf, and Elder had all of the food they needed and all the time they wanted for resting. Having no reason to travel, they were able to enjoy a few days of easy, loafing life around their buffalo mesa. Nonetheless, Shewolf became increasingly restive and began taking long, meandering walks each morning. Not to hunt but in seemingly aimless wandering, exploring the nearby hills and valleys just out of curiosity or because of some private reason. Wolf started to accompany her the first two times, but he sensed that she preferred to be alone.

Elder understood her behavior but avoided the subject in Wolf's presence. It was something for Shewolf to handle. The old dog was thoroughly happy. He took full advantage of the opportunity to doze at will—much of the time. Especially pleased by the active role he had played on the last hunt, he repeatedly complimented Wolf for having planned it so well—even to the point of arranging for placement of the meat in cold storage.

The rising late-afternoon moon was nearly full when Shewolf consumed the last of the bison meat. Lying down next to Wolf that night, she confided that she was anxious to begin preparations for the arrival of their litter. She could feel the unborn whelps growing inside her. And she had seen a small vanguard of Canadian geese flying north two days before. She wanted to move by morning. Wolf lay full length, staring into the distance. He felt a surge of affection—warm, good feelings. In a moment he pulled himself to her and softly rubbed his head against hers. Then he licked her face. This she did not anticipate and his tongue touched her eye directly—before it could close. Eyelid fluttering spasmodically, she turned her head away and stroked it smoothly with a paw to soothe the irritation.

Wolf wedged his muzzle between forelegs, noisily

sniffing the soil in mild embarrassment. An uncontrollable snort caused Elder to glance at them, and Wolf gazed up at silhouetted pine needles. Shewolf rose and shook. Most of the snow is gone from the lower hills. It is time to find a den site. Our valley of the beaver ponds has many good locations—all near water. Again thinking about all that she must do, Shewolf wanted to go immediately. I'm afraid that another group may move in before we return.

Wolf hesitated, then leapt up and stretched with considerable grunting intended as a signal to Elder. But he didn't stir. Wolf ambled to a ponderosa a few feet behind the old dog, and, tail up, roughed his head, neck, and ribs into the bark, cracking off numerous flakes. Elder's eyes opened; his tail was slowly flopping the ground.

Next Wolf marked the trunk and followed this with an inspired performance of the ground-scratching ritual. Dirt flew in all directions, but mostly on Elder. As he raked up a last spray of earth, Wolf dipped, then raised his opening muzzle to voice a brief but emphatic song of one note. Soon the trio was trotting single file in bright moonlight over the undulating plains along the base of the foothills, moving rapidly toward the canyon mouth where the beaver stream emerged from the mountains.

* * *

Bright patches of new green were showing themselves to white and blue sky throughout the valley. Small pastel aspen leaves danced in the mild air to the endless music of spring melting.

Shewolf had dug one burrow near the base of a thinly forested ridge on the south side of the lower valley. The digging had been easy at first as the glacial soil consisted largely of sand and fine gravel. But when she had extended the horizontal tunnel only seven feet, it abutted a cluster of boulders that prevented further deepening. So she clawed out a chamber upward and sideways. It could serve as an alternate den for emergency use, but Shewolf was not satisfied with it as a primary home, the place of whelping. And because she was now more than halfway to that time, the preparation of a proper site became an urgent matter to her.

Not much farther downstream the same moraine ridge arched across the valley describing an elongate horseshoe form around the lower meadows. Shewolf followed it over to the north side, carefully considering each potentially suitable locality. Both Wolf and Elder were reluctant to endorse her eventual selection. It had been the burrow of red foxes in the previous year and still held their alien scent. But that did not bother Shewolf. She would enlarge it and bury lingering odors beneath the entrance mound.

Most of the initial excavating was done by Shewolf: pawing at the floor, walls, and ceiling, and in the awkward task of backing out while scraping loose earth. The fresh entrance mound grew day by day. Like the other den, this one also terminated in an enlarged room against a boulder. But here it was some twelve feet from the entrance, and there was just one obstructing rock. Shewolf determined to circumvent it and deepen the burrow. Edging around the right side of the boulder, she dug a curving extension tunnel which angled slightly upward six feet farther into the hillside and at its end excavated a spacious chamber about four feet in diameter. The entire passageway was even large enough for Wolf and Elder to negotiate comfortably, only requiring a semicrouch in the more constricted places.

The moon was new again when the den was completed. Many times each day thereafter Shewolf would inspect it, rarely leaving the immediate vicinity. Her longest and most frequent forays were to the tributary stream which skirted the horseshoe ridge just over its rounded crest to the north. The easiest route was through a low saddle approximately fifty yards to the left of the den, and she soon had padded a visible path to water.

The responsibility of hunting fell to Wolf and Elder alone. Shewolf would not accompany them for many weeks. Elder invariably mustered enough energy to stay with Wolf for the first few hours but then would tire noticeably and undertake a thorough search of a small central area as his younger companion ranged outward in long loops. Early one starlit morning Wolf made his most important discovery since returning to their valley: two winter-killed yearling elk. They lay side by side partially submerged beneath a thin crust of night ice at the upstream corner of a beaver dam. Although bloated, their meat was palatably fresh. Wolf supposed that they had recently broken through an insubstantial crust and helplessly frozen to death or drowned—perhaps during one of the heavy spring snows.

Working together he and Elder finally managed to drag the two carcasses partway onto a low, muddy bank. Immediately they began the long process of shuttling portions four miles to the den area. The first of these they tendered to Shewolf. Then, after feeding themselves and resting by the dam, they carried all else that they could secure in their mouths back to be buried. The caches were made simply by raking out shallow hollows and covering the food with loosened earth by sweeping motions of their muzzles. The new provisions would not last long, but they helped to put Shewolf at ease and relieve the heavy pressure of contant hunting.

Shewolf was now remaining near the den for longer and longer periods. Sometimes she would lie facing out of the entrance, staring to infinity and panting

softly. And often she was secluded in one of the interior chambers.

Elder had found what he considered to be an ideal resting spot for use when not hunting. A shaded flat among the trees, it lay just below the ridgecrest overlooking the burrow and commanded a good view of most of the lower meadows. He would return from hunting excursions in a state approaching total exhaustion. Dragging himself up to his place, he would then flop to the ground and sleep for hours without moving. Wolf too was often near collapse, but he stayed awake as long as he could guarding the den. And even though he knew that Shewolf was inside not far behind him, he missed her physical presence.

* * *

Spring flies were beginning to hatch and interrupt Elder's midday nap. Reclining against the base of a lodgepole pine, he struggled to hold his temper and ignore the buzzing pests. But when they lit on his graying nose, he could not help swatting at them with a forepaw. After rolling forward in a particularly angry lunge, he became conscious of three magpies pulling and picking at a cache of meat near the bottom of the slope. He launched himself downhill in a determined if somewhat arthritic charge. Crashing through a snag of dead branches, he scattered the screeching birds to nearby trees and sent a chipmunk squeaking off in terror.

Where is Wolf? Straddling a fragrant bit of venison in full-chested defiance, Elder looked around. A flickering motion by the den drew his attention. Wolf's tail! If so close, he must have been aware of the magpies. Elder trotted toward him purposefully.

As the other came into full view, the old dog's gait switched into the frisky bounding of a puppy. Wolf was prone, peering intently into the burrow. Ears forward, his tail was fairly whipping the air. He could see nothing—just a few feet of the tunnel—but his excitement was alive. Elder pressed in next to him. Deep inside Shewolf was crouched, her haunches slightly elevated. And she presented her first tiny whelp to the soft floor of her earthen room. He could not see it, but Elder knew the singular quality of her expression.

Shewolf turned to the newborn pup and delicately removed its protective sac. Then, having snipped the umbilical cord, she carefully cleansed and dried the furry little female before attending to her own needs. In response to a peeping whimper she rolled over on her side and, with her muzzle, gently pushed the sucking whelp into position for nursing. As the puppy fed with a vigorous lunging motion it emitted a soft, rhythmic mewing. Shewolf watched for a while and then rested her head with a tremulous sigh of deep contentment.

Before long she began to feel contractions of the next labor, so she pushed up into her posture of delivery. The nursing pup dangled for a moment, then dropped softly to the floor and began a pleading whine for more milk. Three male puppies came next at intervals of about half an hour. Each time Shewolf rose to whelp, the impatient chorus of whines and whimpers grew louder. Although the sound was very faint at the den entrance, Wolf and Elder could hear it clearly and were able to distinguish each voice. They remained in a state of high excitement—plus growing curiosity. Periodically they looked at each other, wagging their tails more rapidly. By now the scavenging magpies had stripped most of the meat from a deer shoulder which they had removed from its cache.

The fifth whelp was a tiny female, the smallest of all. And this time labor did not start again. A litter of five. Blind, deaf, and helpless, the wooly dark-brown puppies wriggled and clung to their mother's warm body. About the size of chubby ground squirrels, the pups had rounded heads with blunt muzzles and small floppy ears. Their short legs were of little use as yet; they could barely pull along on full stomachs, thin three-inch tails trailing behind. When one wandered away from its mother, sorrowful cries would soon prompt retrieval. The smaller female seemed to lose its way most often.

TWENTY-ONE

For the first few days Shewolf stayed with her litter almost continuously, leaving the den only to relieve herself and for an occasional drink and quick meal of cached meat. The first time she came out Wolf and Elder were still maintaining their vigil, resting by the entrance. They greeted her with unusual emotion and were delighted by her confirmation that all was well. Immediately the two started off to hunt. Wolf almost ached with desire to sing—as a release of nervous excitement and to invoke good fortune for their evening's efforts. But he felt that he could not. Even though the newborn puppies were unable to hear, now that they had come he would enforce his vow to remain silent until such time as they might sing. He was sure, he was *sure* that it would not be very long.

By the end of the litter's first week Shewolf was spending an hour or two each day outside, resting near the entrance with Wolf and Elder. The pups had doubled in weight, and Wolf was becoming increasingly eager to enter the whelping chamber to inspect his progeny. But he would wait for Shewolf's invitation. Elder knew that his introduction would be on the occasion of the puppies' first emergence from the den.

A heavy afternoon rain shower caused Wolf some concern because a considerable amount of water was trickling from the back slope of the entrance mound into the burrow. He waited anxiously for Shewolf's daily appearance. She did not come out until dusk, long after the storm. Vibrations from thunder had frightened the puppies, so she had stayed curled around them until their trembling subsided in deep slumber. She reported that the floor of the tunnel had become muddy as far back as the large boulder, but that no drainage had reached beyond that because of the slight upward incline. The puppies' room was dry.

Several days later Shewolf emerged earlier in the afternoon than usual and, tail swinging, seemed very enthusiastic. Wolf and Elder rushed to meet her. The eyes of three of the pups are beginning to open! She-wolf was holding her head quite high in unrestrained pride. And they're playing a little bit, batting each other with front paws and nibbling ears and tails. Elder and Wolf had heard a few faint yelps at the burrow entrance and suspected that they signaled diminutive mock battles. Shewolf's expression suddenly changed to alert concern and her eyes followed along the ridgecrest above the den. Black-bear scent. Wolf walked to face her.

The bear traveled along our watering stream on the other side of the ridge sometime early this morning. We scented him immediately when we returned from the hunt. I followed the trail for a long distance but didn't meet him. He's a mature boar. He must have moved on up the valley.

In spite of this reassurance, Shewolf was still uneasy and again surveyed the top of the pine-fringed moraine. Then she trotted back to the den and disappeared inside. Wolf had thought that this day he might be able to visit the litter. He was disappointed. He and Elder started on their hunt early.

* * *

Wolf sensed immediately that at long last he would meet his puppies. Something in Shewolf's manner told him as she loped over to his shady bed of pine needles. Elder quickly trotted in to join them. All puppies' eyes were now fully open. Two, the first female and the middle male, had even learned to stand and take a few shaky steps. Shewolf was beaming.

It won't be long until they'll be able to come outside for short periods. Shewolf's sore teats reminded her to add that the whelps had grown a few front teeth. Sharp ones.

They're awake and playing now. And she walked back toward the den, looking over her shoulder to Wolf. He jumped up and almost butted her from the rear in his zeal to follow her inside. He could hear feeble growling from the playing pups. But she wanted him to wait long enough for her to greet and give them the security of her presence before meeting their father for the first time. She glanced at one of the cache sites and suggested that he bring in some pieces of deer skin for the puppies to chew as an aid in teething. All they had at present to massage their gums was each other and Shewolf.

Upon hearing a low whimper from his mate, Wolf lunged into the tunnel, a few strips of hide hanging from his mouth. Having forgotten its dimensions in his excitement, he bumped his head on the roof just inside the entrance, causing a minor cave-in. Elder was peering in behind him with a gray, stoical expression —but a wagging tail. The floor of the tunnel was still damp as far as the boulder. Unaccustomed to the darkness of the burrow, Wolf could see nothing. Moving cautiously now in a low crouch, his chest brushed bottom in several of the more confined stretches. As he rounded the boulder and approached the puppies' room he could hear animated whimpers and yelps. He became highly nervous. It seemed that his heart was louder than the puppy sounds.

In a moment the tunnel widened so that Wolf was able to stand erect. He felt Shewolf's muzzle press against his face. Soon after depositing his gifts of deer skin, Wolf heard agitated growls and tiny shuffling feet: three puppies were struggling with a piece of hide. One by one they became aware of his presence, either by colliding with him, sensing his body heat, or perhaps by scent. When he lay down they clustered around and received him with affectionate abandon, pawing and licking about his head and whimpering softly. He was overcome by unknown feelings.

Although the air was heavy with the smells of Shewolf and the pups, their chamber seemed relatively clean. As if to demonstrate the art of den cleanliness, Shewolf rolled the older female pup to its back and stroked its exposed stomach with her tongue. This caused the whelp to eliminate, and its mother then proceeded to consume all waste, following the means of sanitary control that is natural to many denning creatures.

At length Wolf rose again and, bending his head low, thoroughly sniffed his offspring, nuzzling and nibbling each one. After letting them greet him one more time, he accepted a signal from his mate and departed. Very slowly. He did not want to leave his family so soon, but by the time he saw light from the entrance, he could hardly wait to describe his experience for Elder.

* * *

The morning sky was bright, almost cloudless. A yellow-shafted flicker was diligently attempting to secure something in the grass by thrusting its long, pointed beak in rapid woodpecker motion. Then it would pause, shake its head, and stab again. Insects were now numerous: flies buzzing everywhere—especially near the wolves' food stores; a few bees investigating the colorful display of wild flowers among the green at the base of the den ridge.

The scene changed abruptly as Shewolf strode slowly from her burrow followed by one, then two staggering, squinting wolf pups. This galvanized Wolf and Elder to action. Scrambling to their feet in the shade of nearby lodgepoles, they galloped toward the den. The flicker was flapping rapidly away, exhibiting the rabbit-like white spot at the base of its tail.

A third puppy wobbled out and flopped to its stomach while attempting to scramble up the entrance mound. The final pair soon followed, and all five stood unsteadily, blinking in silent bewilderment before the bright, verdant universe of mountain springtime. Elder and Wolf slowed to a walk as they approached so as not to frighten the uncertain pups. Shewolf seated herself to the left of the entrance and proudly looked down at her litter. The admiring sire and adopted grandfather stopped a few feet from the whelps and, like Shewolf, simply watched them. The first opportunity actually to see the cause of their long excitement and delight. They were completely captivated. And for Elder it was even more special—his introduction.

In a few moments the puppies began to move, taking cautious steps and bobbing their heads slightly as they sniffed and cast about in wonder. Two were whimpering. After considered observation, Elder decided upon appropriate means of referring to the individual pups: the larger female, the first whelp, would be Sister; the first and smallest male, Brother; the middle male, Black, because of the very dark fur on his back; the last male, the largest whelp of the litter, Brown; and the smaller female, the last and smallest whelp, Runty.

Shewolf and Wolf expressed mixed reactions to these suggestions. No puppy of hers would be referred to as Runty. By far the most striking characteristic of the little female was her one pale blue eye: therefore, Blue-eye. And Wolf, asserting that Brown was both unimaginative and indistinctive inasmuch as all five were clothed in brown puppy fur, insisted upon Little

Dirus for the largest male. Pleased that three of his offerings had been accepted and feeling unable to question the preferences of the whelps' parents, Elder agreed to these changes although he was less enthusiastic about the latter one.

It soon became obvious that the whelps were now able to hear, for they would turn toward or waddle to one another in response to whines and yelps. Unable to restrain themselves any longer, Wolf and Elder finally padded forward to examine each pup. Wolf let Elder make his rounds first and, although Wolf had already been introduced, they greeted Elder with equally as much affectionate licking, nibbling, and pawing. And the old dog made no effort to disguise his willingness to accept the role of doting grandfather. Just like the adults', the puppies' tails were all wagging.

TWENTY-TWO

The first time the pups ventured outside, Shewolf guided them back into the burrow after a very short time. But each day thereafter they remained in their grassy nursery longer, and each day their physical abilities and adjustment to this new world improved markedly. They now ranged in weight from six to eight pounds, and their legs grew stronger and steadier with exercise. They were able to scamper and jump through the grass, romping and playing, and to climb up on the entrance mound.

With use they gained control of their eyes and could focus on nearby objects—sticks to chew with an increasing number of puppy teeth—each other, leading to endless chases and ambushes. In these tussles the whelps were beginning the struggle to establish an order of dominance in the litter.

During their fourth daily period of activity in front of the den, Shewolf rose from her resting place by the entrance and walked straight to Black and Sister, who were tugging and shaking on opposite ends of a piece of sinew. The ever-proud mother seemed to be even more pleased than usual by her litter's rapid development. Wolf and Elder looked up sleepily. To their surprise, Shewolf carefully picked up Black in her jaws, his head and forelegs hanging from one side of her mouth, tail and hind legs from the other, and trotted toward them. Just before reaching the resting adults, Shewolf turned to prance by in front of them, tail high and wagging. It was a private exhibition, a showing-off of her wonderful puppies. She circled around the entire perimeter of the grassy flat before returning Black to his play. Then she gently seized Sister and repeated the performance. The program continued until all five puppies had had their showing.

In addition to chewing, chasing, and wrestling, exploration of their vast domain—flowers, insects, pine cones, the anatomies of each other and the mature members of the family—also consumed much of the puppies' time outside the den. Perhaps because they were with her so much in the den, the pups seemed to concentrate these investigations on Wolf and Elder in preference to their mother. Especially on Elder, who, unlike their father, did not visit them in their chamber. Elder's tolerance of needle-teeth biting, sniffing, crawling, and general harassment seemed almost unlimited—greater than Wolf's—but even he would occasionally have to move to privacy beyond the nursery limits established by Shewolf. All of this intimate contact between the whelps and adults during their outside hours led to the development of very strong emotional attachments within the family, ties and needs that would form the basis of group unity in the puppies' future lives.

Although the smallest, Blue-eye was also the most agile, and the first pup to attempt stalking prey other than her littermates, usually grasshoppers whose noisy rasping caught her attention. The fact that her clumsy pounces were rarely successful never diminished her enthusiasm. These hapless onslaughts revealed her natural hunting instincts that would be developed by the examples of her elders when she began to accompany them some six months later.

The pups were now large enough to nurse standing up next to and underneath Shewolf, and whenever she moved at least one of them always seemed to be following her or lunging up for another meal. But increasingly Shewolf would refuse to serve on demand. The long, gradual process of weaning had begun. To encourage this necessary transition, all three adults occasionally regurgitated well-digested food for the puppies to sample. Before long all of their meat would be presented in this manner.

In the fifth week the puppies' ears began to rise. Little Dirus and Sister had halfway ears, the tips still floppy. The other pups started one at a time: one ear partly up, one droopy. This gave them all an especially mischievous appearance, which was well suited to their behavior. Their eyes rolled in all directions. Now ranging in weight from eight to eleven pounds, they continued to grow very rapidly. Accordingly, Shewolf extended the boundaries of the nursery from the immediate environs of the den entrance to the periphery of the surrounding grassy flat.

* * *

Gray clouds recalling winter cold had pushed in during the previous night. The afternoon sky was heavy with low overcast. Although above freezing, the air was the coldest the puppies had known and, rather than inhibit their activity, it made them even more frisky than usual. Stalking, chasing, and wrestling continued almost uninterrupted and, for the first time, these endless play struggles began to confirm the dominance that had been subtly developing in the litter since the pups had first emerged from the den.

Blue-eye and Little Dirus had been engaged in a prolonged series of ambushes and rough-and-tumble in-fighting. Although Little Dirus was much larger and stronger, Blue-eye was quicker and consistently avoided his headlong charges and flattening pounces. Instead, she was able to thrust under him, grab an opposite-side paw, and pull him to his back with a thump. As Little Dirus picked himself up after suffering one such indignity, his littermate rose on trembling hind legs and laid her forepaws across his shoulders, signifying dominance. None of her littermates was able to get the better of Blue-eye. However, Black was generally overpowered by Little Dirus but in turn held sway over Brother. Sister participated in paired battles less than the others, often being relegated to solitary spectating. She usually submitted too quickly and easily to offer satisfying competition. The energetic capers were accompanied by ever louder and more diverse puppy sounds: would-be fierce growls, spontaneous yaps, whimpers, and lengthening whines.

One afternoon while investigating mysterious shadows at the edge of the trees, Blue-eye was overcome by her boundless curiosity and stalked cautiously into the unfamiliar world beyond the nursery. But before long she was lost—and lonely. Then frightened. Raising her one-ear-floppy head, she opened her mouth to voice a lengthy yowling whine. Wolf had been sleeping, but this sound pierced him. He was standing rigid and shivering. The first sign.

* * *

An ill-guarded mule-deer fawn was the hunt's only reward that night. As Wolf and Elder approached the den in predawn light, they sensed that something was wrong even before they smelled the bear. Hackles bristled. Wolf dropped the haunch he was carrying and stretched into full run. The same boar black bear that had followed their watering stream. Heavy scent all around—from the ridge, several caches. At the den entrance! Jolting to a halt, Wolf sent a low call to his mate. There was no reply, so he scrambled into the burrow. It was empty.

TWENTY-THREE

Elder was waiting for Wolf when he came dashing back out. I found their trail. It crosses the bear's and angles straight toward the other side of the valley. Shewolf has returned and reused it several times. She must've carried the pups to the other den.

Did the bear follow?

He went back over the ridge. Relieved by this news, Wolf shook vigorously to throw off soil he had scraped loose on his frantic round trip to the whelping chamber. Although they were both very tired after a long night of hunting, the two wolves immediately broke into a fast lope along Shewolf's trail. They would return later for their jettisoned venison.

The sky had cleared overnight. Orange light in the east promised imminent sunrise as Wolf and Elder approached the alternate den. Shewolf was lying in the entrance. Forgetting himself momentarily, Wolf's call of greeting was sufficiently long and loud as to suggest a brief song. But his emotion was understood. Shewolf trotted out to meet them, giving her special squeak. All puppies were well and sleeping heavily in their new chamber after an unexpectedly exciting night.

When Shewolf had first scented the bear from inside the den it was digging up one of their meat caches. She had rushed out and charged. It was easy to dodge the boar's heavy lunges and paw swipes. Then after a few minutes of circling and parrying, the bear grabbed some deer ribs and lumbered off. Shewolf stood guard outside the den for a long time before rejoining her sleeping litter.

Later the bear's odor had come again, much stronger. He was sniffing around the den entrance. This time Shewolf waited inside, greatly disturbed and frightened. It was then that she had decided to move the pups. As soon as he had gone she quickly inspected the surrounding area and set about transferring the whelps to their new home, one-by-one in her mouth.

The puppies remained sleeping until late in the

day and so had an abbreviated play period outside. The adult wolves also slept much. Wolf had returned to the former den site several times to retrieve some of the cached meat plus that obtained on the previous night's hunt before he himself collapsed finally into slumber.

The unseasonably cold temperatures of the day before had moderated to pleasant coolness under the mid-afternoon sun. Elder was still asleep. Wolf and Shewolf were lying just a few feet apart watching their offspring cautiously explore their wondrous new nursery. They seemed less steady on their feet than in previous days. Now nearly a foot long and disproportionately big, their legs had been growing so fast that at times coordination did not seem to be keeping pace. Wolf's long nap had relaxed and refreshed him. He recalled Blue-eye's song-like whine and wondered how soon he might hear it again.

Shewolf had been aware of Wolf's reaction to Blue-eye's whine, so she felt obliged to inform him of an instruction she had given the puppies shortly after their arrival at the new den. She had been badly frightened by the bear's visit, especially because it was the second time he had passed through the area. She did not want to risk his approaching their new home unexpectedly, particularly now that the pups were spending so much time outside. Consequently she had discouraged them from making unnecessary loud noise for a while—such puppy sounds could be heard at considerable distance and might reveal the location of their den. She hoped that the marauder would soon leave the vicinity.

Wolf didn't think that this precaution was necessary or even effective inasmuch as scent could betray them just as easily and at any time of day, but he did not communicate this opinion in deference to Shewolf's maternal concern for the litter's safety. Nonetheless, the situation bothered him. He felt that the time for the emergence of song in the pups was very near, and he feared that this restriction on their free expression by voice, mild as it was, might inhibit or even prevent singing.

Perhaps there is a brief, critical time when the urge surfaces. Then or never. He rolled over on his side, attempting to conceal his anxiety. The thought crossed his mind that Shewolf could be using the bear as an excuse to retard the development of song because of her fear that singing would increase the danger of attack by other wolves. But he didn't believe that. He hoped that it was not so.

Trilling, chir-like cries that evening announced the return of the nighthawks for the warm season. Swooping and darting on long, white-patched wings and fluttering in erratic, bat-like rolls, they crisscrossed the dusk sky in pursuit of flying insects.

On the next afternoon the puppies again enjoyed

a full period outside. Most of it was given to thorough exploration of the nursery. Some discoveries, however, led to brief struggles, as when Black and Brother engaged in a lively, growling tug-of-war with a small branch. Black finally made off with the prize and lay down to strip its bark and shred the wood with great sense of purpose. One or more of the pups would often waddle after any of the adult wolves that moved through their play area, learning the practice of following which they would later put to use when traveling with the group. Wolf noticed that the level of puppy noise was indeed lower than before. There were no loud whines.

By the end of two more weeks the weaning process had advanced considerably. Shewolf was making herself available for nursing much less than before. Instead, disgorged, relatively fresh meat was regularly being furnished to the litter chiefly by Shewolf but also by Wolf and occasionally Elder. The puppies were gradually learning to consume this new food, tearing off small pieces like bark from sticks with their growing front teeth. Soon they began to ask for solid food from adults returning from hunting or from caches by licking and pawing at their elders' mouths in order to initiate and stimulate regurgitation.

This transition in the whelps' diet required an increased supply of meat. Wolf was taking his hunting duties more seriously than ever before, going out for

longer times and ranging farther. As the demands on physical endurance increased, Elder's role in scouting and actual hunting diminished. His contribution now was made mainly in helping Wolf transport and cache food. The black bear had not returned so their stores were largely undisturbed except for minor but bothersome thievery by the ubiquitous magpies and gray jays, and an occasional raven.

* * *

The puppies continued to grow at a remarkable rate; changes were noticeable almost daily. All ears were now erect, and the pups' weights ranged from the twelve pounds of Blue-eye to Little Dirus' seventeen. Their heads and paws looked abnormally large for their bodies. Shewolf had again expanded the approved limits of the nursery to include a few of the nearer cache sites. Wolf first realized that Shewolf had also canceled her restrictions on puppy sound as a result of an incident at one of these caches.

While the other four were gamboling in the grass, Sister had slipped away to investigate a fragrant burial place. After much digging and tugging, she stood very much pleased with herself clenching a length of deer intestine in her dirt-speckled mouth. Her excavating, however, had attracted the attention of Little Dirus who scampered over and grabbed away the choice tidbit, shaking it violently. Deprived of her rightful treasure,

Sister backed away yipping and yapping. And then raised her head partway upward and voiced an undulating, trailing whine of frustration. Wolf was a quarter of a mile away. He heard it. He might have been standing at Sister's side.

It happened again the next day. A scraping noise and the snapping of sticks heralded Brother's entrance from the trees dragging an enormous branch by one end. He was making an awkward effort at prancing, but the stubborn limb wouldn't let him and caused him repeatedly to stumble and occasionally fall, losing his grip. Black was watching with ears erect, brown eyes shining, and an expression of mischievous intensity. At once he bounded forward and, swinging his head up to the side, emitted a long ah-rooo. With that he charged the stumbling Brother and knocked him flat. Wolf was resting close by with Elder. His expression was every bit as intense as Black's had been. They're starting to sing. Almost.

Elder did not raise his head. No, no, they're just whining and yowling as puppies sometimes do. He looked up at Wolf. Because this is so important to you, wait for unmistakable singing—if it ever happens. And Elder issued a lengthy sigh from the side of his mouth, causing his lip to flap rhythmically.

Despite Elder's reaction, Wolf was confident that the puppy calls were the forerunners of true singing. But he took the old dog's advice. He wanted there to be no doubt. In the days that followed, life around the den became more vocal even than before the move to the alternate den. Yips and yaps; whines and whimpers; yowls, growls, and barks. The blossoming energy of growth was released to the accompaniment of incessant, clamorous puppy sound. And from among these varied vocal expressions, Wolf distinguished more and more frequently the long trailing whine that was almost song. Each day he expected to hear full, undeniable puppy singing.

Two mornings later a light, warm breeze flowing down from the peaks to the west rose into a roaring gale that gusted furiously through that day and into the next. No sooner had it started than the long puppy whines which Wolf regarded as early singing ceased altogether. He became distressed, haunted by the conclusion that the time for song development had passed. More depressed than in a long time, he started off to hunt in late afternoon. He went alone and was unsuccessful.

The next afternoon the wind subsided and shifted to a cool flow from the east carrying a layer of low cloud. As the overcast evening sky darkened, Wolf and Elder began to stir in preparation for their nightly hunt. The food supply was low. This time they would stay out until they replenished it.

Now almost two months old, the pups were staying out until dark. This evening they were still in the nursery and showing unusual interest in the restlessness and tail wagging of Wolf and Elder as they were about to depart. The pups danced around them, rearing on hind legs and excitedly licking muzzles as if trying to induce a regurgitated meal. They sensed that a hunt was about to begin.

Gliding silently through the gloom somewhere near, a great horned owl sounded its ghostly voice. Oo-oo, oo-oo! All of the puppies turned in one motion and held their breaths to listen to the call of an unknown creature. Then Blue-eye bravely lifted her petite, bewhiskered muzzle to the sky, squeezed her eyelids tightly shut, and sang out in a series of lengthening yowls and whines. Her notes rose and fell in high pitched ululation. Not a single phrase, but one after the other for many seconds. The others were transfixed. Emotion rose in Wolf uncontrollably.

Little Dirus was not to be outdone. He followed his littermate's example, swinging his nose up vertically and parting his jaws to contribute a prolonged wowing yodel of slightly lower pitch. Black and Brother started almost simultaneously: two feeble sirens straining for identity. The four puppy voices intertwined in a chorus of beautifully sincere, spontaneous expression. Only Sister failed to join their singing.

But all ceased in mid-breath the instant that Wolf's long-imprisoned voice burst into the night in full impassioned song. The feelings he released in this moment surpassed any that he had known before. Elder and Shewolf had never heard him sing with such force and sensitivity. His very spirit seemed to be flowing with his voice.

As his song tempered very gradually in descent, the four puppies began their chorus anew. Even more excited than the first time, many yaps and squeals now mingled with their longer calls. Then another voice joined them: louder and more mature but completely uncontrolled in vibrant oscillations and rolling breaks. A bolt of energy surged to the extremes of Wolf's nerves. He looked down to see Shewolf standing next to Sister, singing encouragement to her one silent puppy. Suddenly Sister cried out in surprisingly pure tones. All that Wolf could possibly do in his dimensionless emotion was to give himself in his voice, and he joined the family chorus. At seven weeks of age, five little wolves were singing freely with their parents. Something new—yet very ancient.

Elder absorbed the scene in silence. Not the silence of disapproval, but of reverence. For now he knew that Wolf had been right, that Wolf had experienced the truth. To his relief, Elder was finally able to listen in unqualified appreciation. The proud old dog knew that he himself could never sing. And for this he was profoundly sad.

TWENTY-FOUR

The night after the puppies fully realized the joy of expression in song, Shewolf joined Wolf on his hunting excursion. Elder stayed behind to guard the den. As they ranged upvalley together toward the place where Wolf had last located elk, the two quietly enjoyed the pure appreciation they shared for their existence. And Shewolf confided to him that her reaction to singing had been just as moving and basic to her as any experience of her life. It had aroused a part of her spirit that she had not known.

Two weeks later the family vacated their den and moved four miles farther up the valley, closer to a large concentration of elk in higher meadows. The pups were now more than two months old and no longer required the security of a burrow. Instead Shewolf selected a grassy terrace at the edge of trees above the stream as a sort of rendezvous. Clumps of willows and a few young lodgepole pines were scattered across the flat, affording many hiding places. The puppies stayed here with at least one adult most of the time, and soon it was crisscrossed by trails. Within a week the grass and bushes were showing signs of heavy wear and tear.

The puppies were beginning to grow a little adult hair in shades of gray to black—and a trace of rusty yellow. It appeared first on their elongating faces, then on their bodies. Ever larger, even Blue-eye now stood fourteen inches at the shoulder and weighed almost twenty pounds. Her practice on grasshoppers paid its first reward late one afternoon when she pounced on a mouse as it scurried from its grass-sheltered burrow intent on a little evening nibbling. Blue-eye had fed herself for the first time. All of the pups became notorious throughout the neighborhood for their inclination to charge anything that moved, provided that it was not too large.

By the time they were four months old, the family had moved to a second but similar rendezvous in somewhat less used condition half a mile upstream. The loss of puppy teeth was frustrating and sometimes slightly painful, but this had been at least partly compensated for by the filling out of proud bushy tails.

Elder hunted only irregularly now, usually staying in or near the rendezvous close to the pups. Each evening the family enjoyed a group song session in the time of excitement prior to the departure of Wolf and Shewolf in search of food. Because each wolf could easily distinguish the voices of the others, song soon became a useful way of communicating location at a distance, as when separated while hunting or upon returning to the rendezvous.

After having seriously misinterpreted the direction from which Shewolf's song had come on a gusty hunting night, Wolf finally realized the reason for the silence of the puppies during those windy days just as they were about to sing for the first time. Wind confuses the signals of direction and distance, thereby lessening the advantages of song in communication—even to the point of disadvantage. The pups' silence had expressed a lesson perpetuated in the past. Wolf now knew that it had actually been a positive sign, a sign that their minds held the rules of singing.

At six months of age Little Dirus stood twenty-four inches at the shoulder and weighed seventy pounds. All of the pups looked like somewhat small, gangling adults. Their winter coats had filled out, and their adult incisors fully erupted. Canine teeth were at least half-grown. By now the pattern of cold-season storms had again developed and was beginning to dominate the shortening, less frequent periods of mild weather. Deer and elk were assembling in larger groups and slowly migrating to lower elevations as snow began to accumulate in the high country.

During a gentle evening snowfall, a final chorus of song signaled a seasonal farewell to their mountain valley and the third rendezvous of Blue-eye, Little Dirus, Black, Brother, and Sister. Henceforth the entire family would hunt together, ranging among the foothills and high plains until spring. At twenty-two months the young wolves would be fully mature, and by then most of them would strike out on their own, alone or perhaps in pairs. And so they lived for six more years.

TWENTY-FIVE

In the seventh spring of the pair, Shewolf was barren. Her time of motherhood had ended. She and Wolf had reared thirty-five whelps. Their last litter, now six yearling wolves, was hunting with them. Elder had lived for three of those years. But the affectionate care and attention of his adopted family could not stay the effects of a long and full life indefinitely. Early one arctic morning, his body was cold. Gazing silently at him still curled tightly in his sleeping position, Wolf and Shewolf could almost hear, could feel the rasping of his familiar snore. For a long time thereafter Wolf's song was unusually restrained, sounding very much like a lament.

The valley of the beaver dams and elk meadows had become the center of their warm-season territory. It was known to wolves at great distance. Generally in the first years as an encampment of debased or deranged wolves, then as the place of the strange ones. With time its reputation softened further. The singing valley. A colony of singing wolves. The annual litter of whelps plus lingering immature wolves maintained the group's numbers at about twelve. And each year a few young wolves would enter the valley in their search for home territory. Some stayed and learned to sing. A few of these remained in the region, but most eventually moved on, dispersing throughout the mountains and plains as did Wolf's and Shewolf's own offspring.

* * *

Against the white-gray of a monumental thunderhead, Wolf and Shewolf watched the osprey dive and rise from the pond, a trout impaled by its talons. The ripples spread. Wolf gazed at the enlarging circles for many moments without moving. Shewolf sensed his compelling need. She turned to him. Go now. Go to see—and to listen. They looked long into each other's eyes and touched moist noses softly. Then Wolf moved away. He traveled ninety miles in three days.

The early summer night was warm for the high

country. Heavy, tepid, and without noise. Electric. Ethereal curtains of pale scarlet and chartreuse shimmered in the northern sky. Wolf watched from atop a craggy spur just below timberline, silhouetted against the aurora. It pulsed in vibrant, mysterious animation. As if in resonance, he tingled and quivered. Although he had never witnessed this strange cosmic phenomenon, Wolf was happy beneath it. He knew that it belonged to the night.

He glanced at stunted spruce hugging the steep slope. Their diminutive branches reached to the east, awaiting the sun. Proud pennants proclaiming survival of lifelong challenge by the wind. Two thousand feet below, the black ribbon of a meltwater stream meandered intricately down a broad glacial valley. This part of the mountains was new to Wolf. He felt the endless beauty of the earth and breathed deeply. Had this night a special scent?

Without signal, his senses alerted. He looked to the sky; his ears opened and strained to the point of imagining sound. He tensed. He could feel it coming. And then it was there. The song of a wolf. Distant, but excitingly distinct. A wolf of these mountains. A stranger of uncertain ancestry and unknown territory. The song was answered by another, then another. And soon a polychromatic counterpoint of lupine music was playing into the aurora, swirling and diffusing through Wolf's consciousness.

He more than listened and watched. Wolf absorbed. He longed to join the singing, but he could not even try. This was not his time or place. Yet his satisfaction was enormous, consuming—complete. For a few moments. There came slowly an indefinable hollowness, a profound emptiness. A rare inner void known only to those who live for a purpose and suddenly realize its fulfillment.

He looked around and stood listening uneasily a while longer. Then he started down a game path. He would find a place to rest. Smells of bighorn sheep in the cirque. And a mountain grizzly. The ewes and lambs were bedded down on grassy benches scattered amongst the talus. But the grizzly was moving—upslope. Toward Wolf.

At first he froze, then turned and reclimbed the ridge. He positioned himself some fifty yards up the divide from the path, largely out of sight in rocks above the cliff of the cirque wall. From this vantage point he could see most of the ascending trail and the saddle where it crossed the ridgecrest.

His pupils dilated to maximum as he strained to see motion between the dark trees below. There was none, but that familiar odor was stronger. Ears rigidly forward, nose in constant play, Wolf thought that he heard a muffled snort, the clatter of small stones. His pulse jolted when the bear emerged from the shadows, shuffling and sniffing unhurriedly but inexorably upward. Two first-year cubs bounced along behind.

As they approached the pass, the grizzlies moved out of view behind a boulder. Wolf could have stepped cautiously around the corner, but with impulsive bravado he sprang instead to the top of the obstructing rock. He staggered slightly and had to scramble to gain a foothold. This abrupt motion on the skyline caught the attention of the sow's beady eyes.

Rearing on massive hind legs, the great beast raised its wriggling nose eight feet into the air. She turned toward Wolf, eyes rolling to the side in an insanely wild expression. His scent still lay along the ridge. Mother grizzly dropped to all fours and with an unequivocal growl dispatched the scampering cubs into a clump of squat trees. In an instant she was galloping ponderously up the divide. And with deceptive speed. Her head was low, swaying from side to side. She was uttering a jostling, guttural roar.

Wolf had little time to make his escape. He could probably outrun the bear across the spur and downhill—away from her cubs. But he hesitated. He looked over his shoulder. Dared he jump back down the way he had come? No—it was too close to the edge. His momentum might carry him over the cliff. A spasm of fear bolted through his upper body. Somehow he knew that he was now on his own. He no longer felt the sense of protection that had been with him so long.

The grizzly rampaged past Wolf's boulder without locating him. But, suddenly having lost his trail, she wheeled with a deafening bellow and charged, flattening a little spruce.

Wolf's rock was not quite high enough. Again standing upright, the bear lunged at his feet. He danced away from her gnashing teeth, then leapt vertically over the sweep of her devastating forepaw. The force of the blow was so great that she momentarily lost her balance. Wolf began to feel trapped. In mortal danger. He shuddered; his hair bristled.

The grizzly rushed angrily back and forth at the base of Wolf's bastion, rising as she turned and emitting deep, tremulous growls. The next attack was imminent.

In this predicament, how could he outmaneuver and elude the great humpback bear, the supremely confident monarch of the mountains? Only in surprise. Of course! At once Wolf's spirit ignited—flamed. It was no less than that of the Bear! His eyes seemed incandescent. The urge to run, the wisdom of retreat, had transformed into the universal, instinctive determination to fight when cornered, to resist destruction even in the face of overwhelming odds. But much more than this, Wolf was overcome by an obsessive belief in his personal incarnation of wolves' ancient pride, and a compulsion for once to transcend the evolved order of animal dominance. Taut and trembling, he stood poised for defense.

In avoiding the second thrust, Wolf launched himself up and forward. His timing was exact. Landing squarely on the sow's head and upper back as she was still following through, he reached over and sank his canine teeth into her sensitive, juicy nose. The roar that followed was beyond all Wolf's experience.

With a sudden, violent bow of her head, she smashed him into the ground. Stunned, he did not let go. Instead he responded by shaking his own head with all of his remaining strength. The bear was literally blind with rage. Wolf thought that he could stand the pain and the noise but not that awful ursine breath.

Spinning her body completely around, the infuriated grizzly yanked her head in a long upward arc with all the power of her immense barrel neck. As he was cast skyward, Wolf felt his grip yielding. He gave his head a final shake. She would remember him. Old Loose Nose would. And Wolf was propelled up, out, and over the precipitous cirque wall.

Down. Down. Down. He hurtled through the night air, accelerating and spinning. Stars, aurora, mountain, and forest wheeled around and around, faster and faster. He passed through a trace of Bubo's scent. The great horned owl. He could not remember having met him so high before. Wolf tucked in his tail and folded his paws to spin ever faster. His world became a twirling, dazzling whirlpool.

As he closed his eyes, the eddy darkened and blended into its vortex. There was a light. Two lights:

glowing, growing. Amber lights in a black circle. Sort of—head-shaped. It . . . it is a head. Dirus! Standing. A magnificent wolf!

Moist black nose held high. Furrowed. An infinitely complex pattern of skin. Gray guard hairs. Frosted. Each one erect but divergent. Each one with dignity, nobility, and pride. And the eyes! Those burning, penetrating eyes.

Dirus had never been so vividly real, so close, so vital. Wolf knew that for the very first time he was *with* Dirus. He was. . . . He had joined the past.

Ageless granite boulders swallowed his body. And the Universe expanded a little—once again.